THE TURN OF THE TIDE

In the North Cornish village of Penarren, widow Jenny Hawke and her family struggle to keep The Chough café going. When Kit Venning returns, causing controversy, Jenny, unexpectedly, falls in love with him. Then Kit joins the crew of the lifeboat *Etta Trelawney*. It takes dramatic events at sea and the rescue of Jenny's grandson, Ben, to settle past difficulties between the Trelawneys and Vennings . . . and to help Jenny and Kit realise what they mean to each other.

PENELOPE ALEXANDER

THE TURN OF THE TIDE

Complete and Unabridged

LINFORD
Leicester

First published in Great Britain in 2009

First Linford Edition
published 2011

British Library CIP Data

Alexander, Penelope.
 The turn of the tide.- -
(Linford romance library)
1. Widows- -England- -Cornwall (County)- -
Fiction. 2. Lifeboat crew members- -England- -
Cornwall (County)- -Fiction. 3. Love stories.
4. Large type books.
I. Title II. Series
823.9′2–dc22

ISBN 978–1–4448–0686–1

The Chough Café

'Let me climb up, Dad,' Jenny Hawke protested. 'After all, the Chough is my café.'

'I still say it's better I go first,' Garron insisted, gazing skywards with narrowed eyes. 'I need to see exactly what's causing the trouble.'

'I'll fetch the step-ladder, then . . . ' Jenny whisked away before she got another lecture on maintenance and repair. Her dad was a dear, but they seldom agreed first time on anything.

She hauled the tall step-ladder out of her store cupboard, and then dragged it between the double doors of the kitchen and across every bump on the uneven floorboards.

Cool, damp sea air rushed into her face as Garron Trelawney opened the outer door.

'Let me help, Jenny,' he offered. 'You

1

don't have to do everything yourself, you know!'

'It's at times like these that I miss Dan.' She gasped, letting Garron push the step-ladder into place. 'It doesn't seem like ten years since he died, Dad.'

Garron patted his daughter's arm. They all missed Dan, but he'd have been proud to see how Jenny had coped since his death.

'I reckon we've managed pretty well so far,' he said.

'Now.' He grinned. 'I bet I can fix that old bird quicker than you, Mrs Hawke!'

A gust of wind swept the sand dunes and shifted the chough's grating metal frame, as if to make a point. Garron set his hands on the uprights, and raised his eyebrows. Jenny knew better than to argue.

'All right! You first.' She sighed.

'Pass the oil-can,' Garron said, winking cheerfully. 'I'll only be a mo'!'

The painted crow gazed down. Though his feathers were faded, his eye was still sharp. Beneath his two red feet, Jenny read the familiar encouragement: *Try Our Traditional Cornish Food*.

Her dad climbed to shoulder-height and the steps shuddered.

'The ol' tide's coming in a bit rough this evening.' Garron's unconcerned voice floated over her head.

'You're not up there for the view, Dad!' Jenny said, caught between amusement and exasperation.

The ladder jolted again.

'This oil's no good, Jenny! Get me some grease,' Garron called.

'Come down first, Dad,' Jenny called back. 'I can't leave you swaying six feet off the ground!'

Garron gave a grunt, but obeyed.

'Where's my stuff for releasing rusty hinges?' he asked.

Jenny shook her head.

'What do I always say? If you want something doing . . . '

' . . . Do it yourself!' his daughter finished for him.

It was an old, shared joke.

Garron stomped off, and Jenny, more or less patiently, waited for his return.

'My turn,' she told her father as he came back. 'I'm lighter.'

Garron opened his mouth to protest, and then his face softened.

'I know what that old chough means to you, Jenny . . . Go on . . . I'll hold the ladder.'

Smiling, and wielding a rag, a brush and Garron's 'miracle-in-a-pot', Jenny climbed until she was eye-to-eye with her painted bird.

How different Penarren looked from here. Dabbing away at the metal bracket with the steel brush, Jenny allowed her mind to wander.

After Dan's death, the business had become her responsibility. It had been tough at times and she'd have been lost without her dad's help, and that of her family. Still, she sometimes had to remind Garron who owned this café!

Since his retirement, Garron had become so good at DIY they used to joke that pretty soon he'd have replaced the whole maze of the building bit by bit.

'Then we could change the name, and call it the Penarren Palace!' he'd say, half-joking.

But he knew Jenny could never do that. The Chough café had been run by the Hawke family on this spot for as long as anyone could remember, surviving all that life and the wild westerly gales could throw at it.

The breeze was strengthening now. Balanced on her step-ladder, Jenny had to push her hair away from her face to see the chough more clearly.

'Is it any wonder you look your age, my handsome?' she muttered, leaning forward to clean the crow's faded legs.

There never had been much money for repairs. She was afraid the proper solution for her business was a complete overhaul. Either that, or do the unthinkable and sell up! She greased and swung her battered sign until its hinges ran sweetly against the brackets.

'Are you coming down?' Garron called.

A Plan

Jenny took one last look from her vantage point. Beyond the dunes, the line between sea and sky was navy blue. Figures gathered beside the sturdy grey stones of the lifeboat station, and two lone gulls tumbled in the windy sky above the harbour.

Penarren had a trickle of visitors all year round. Though it was far from summer yet, the tourist season would be on them before they knew it and, as always, the Chough needed to attract its share of customers.

Jenny returned to the ground, a plan already forming in her mind.

She smiled at her father.

'The brass band that played beside the harbour last year was really popular. Everyone enjoyed the singing. I was thinking . . . maybe we should aim to have live music at the Chough. After all, the Merrymaid Inn has been doing it for ages. What do you think, Dad?'

Garron blew out his cheeks doubtfully.

'Reckon the café's big enough?' he asked.

'We could open up the back . . . repair that old terrace beside the river . . . yes, I think it would be OK with a bit of planning and rearrangement.' She shrugged.

'Best pray for good weather, then,' Garron said gloomily. 'The wind blows a fair gust along the creek sometimes. Organising could take longer than you think, and we might need a licence . . . ' He brightened suddenly.

'One good thing: our Gary would be in his element — if he and Kerensa haven't moved away by then . . . '

Jenny nodded.

Perhaps her son could get back in touch with the band he used to sing with before he got married. Yes, they'd start small, but music at the Chough could be fun. Whether it would make financial sense, she would have to wait and see.

Born Romantics

Next afternoon, as the sun gleamed between the clouds rolling up from the cove, Jenny left the café with her father in charge. She paused on the steps outside. Sally Rosewarne came jogging towards her, past a scattering of early holidaymakers in the square.

'Hi!' she said, smiling and slightly out of breath.

'Coming up-along for eggs?' Jenny asked. 'I suppose I could drive, but I'd love a walk to Trenfos Farm. Even more if you come with me, Sal.'

'Think I've done my share of aerobics for today!' Sally grinned, re-tying her frizzing hair where it had escaped its band. 'I could use a walk to cool down. Shall we go by the creek?'

They followed the rough pathway by the shallow inlet where a small river ran into one corner of Penarren. Sally strode ahead, taking care not to slip among the weeds. Squat, overhanging bushes reflected in the water beneath the opposite bank. Reaching the wider stretch of shingle, they were able to walk side by side and resume their chat.

'I've been thinking about trying something new — what would you say to live music at the Chough?' Jenny asked.

Sally frowned.

'It might cost more than it made . . . '

'I've got to think positive, Sal. No-one can expect something for nothing, and the Chough needs to keep up. Perhaps it's too late for this year, but we could plan for next . . . what do you think?'

Sally sighed.

'I worry about you, Jenny,' she said. 'My life seems so uncomplicated beside yours . . . '

'Your life is the one that would tie me in knots, Sal,' Jenny said, smiling at her companion.

'I know you don't think you have

problems — apart from the upkeep of the café,' Sally said. 'But you've got your dad, your son, his wife and your grandson all under one roof, and you're responsible for running a business — I don't know how you manage so well!'

'It's lucky I've got so much help, then, isn't it? I couldn't manage without Dad. Or my daughter-in-law. And, of course, Lily pitches in whenever we're short-handed.'

'Where would Penarren be without Lily Pinch?' Sally said. 'Whereas all I have to deal with . . . '

' . . . Is risking your life on a shout,' Jenny finished. 'I suppose being a member of the lifeboat crew doesn't count as being brave!'

Sally laughed, and lobbed a stone into the water.

'I love being part of all that!' she said. 'And as for danger . . . Well, I reckon the *Etta Trelawney* is the smartest boat this side of the Tamar. You've heard Paul Biddick's now our fully fledged mechanic, haven't you?'

'Yes, he told me. I'm so pleased for him. Mind you, I don't expect that'll make his mum worry about him any the less.'

'I wouldn't like to be left on shore, so I can sympathise with her on that one,' Sally said.

'How are you and Paul getting on now?' Jenny asked. 'As crewmates,' she added quickly, in case Sally's friendship with Paul had hit one of its more volatile patches.

'Paul's been so kind and helpful settling me in with the crew,' Sally said. 'He's a different person on that boat. So calm and professional. It's on shore we have problems!'

'Such as?' Jenny asked.

'He never takes anything I say seriously, Jenny! Of course, he's like that with everyone. I'd say he only shows his grown-up side to you . . .'

'We're not that serious!' Jenny laughed. 'I value Paul's friendship, Sal, but it's never been more than that.'

'He's always talking about you,' Sally said.

Jenny looked bemused.

'So he's not likely to become your true love, then?' her friend teased.

'Maybe I'm too old now I'm a grandmother,' Jenny replied with another smile.

'Rubbish. You Trelawneys are all born romantics, however tough you like to act,' Sally said. 'What are you? Thirty-eight? That's only a few years older than me.'

'I was lucky to find such happiness with Dan,' Jenny said, more seriously. 'I wouldn't count on the same thing happening again. Besides, what with the family and the Chough, I'm run off my feet most of the time!'

'I think Pauley's really fond of you, though,' Sally persisted. 'And not just because you're the widow of his closest friend.'

'What's he been hinting?' Jenny asked curiously.

Sally shook her head.

'You know he'd never admit to anything romantic, not in a million years. But it's just the way he looks sometimes. A bit wistful, maybe.'

Jenny hitched her basket on her arm and laughed outright.

'Sally Rosewarne, all I can say is you've got a vivid imagination! Wistful is not a word I've ever heard anyone use about Pauley Biddick!'

'Well, I suppose you know him better than most.' Sally sighed.

Jenny nodded.

'If he wants to get away from his mum and dad, he knows there's a meal for him at the Chough, and we have been out to see the odd film from time to time.'

'Couldn't you ever have any feelings for him?' Sally asked.

Jenny shook her head.

'I've thought about it sometimes, but that's not how we are. Paul just has this sixth sense if I'm feeling low. He always cheers me up!'

'Same here.' Sally smiled.

A Wanderer Returns

They crossed the river by the old bridge. The slate-roofed farm buildings crouched at the head of the valley, blending so well with their surroundings most visitors hardly knew they were there.

'We're lucky we've still got Trenfos, even if it is a bit of a climb,' Jenny said as they came away carrying the eggs. 'Most smallholdings round here have either had to grow or die.'

'This one wouldn't survive without the supplies it sells to the village for the tourist trade,' Sally said. 'So much seems to depend on that these days.'

She stopped suddenly, her hand on Jenny's arm.

'Isn't that someone by the old house? Look, there's a car parked outside . . . '

Jenny stopped, too. Trenfos House stood slightly apart, overlooking the narrow road that wound downhill back to Penarren. Jenny shaded her eyes with her free hand and peered across the road.

'Looks like it,' she said. 'We'll hear soon enough, knowing the Penarren grapevine.'

'One of the Vennings, maybe. But which one?' Sally mused.

'It could be old Mr Venning. You know, the one who moved away with his wife all that time ago,' Jenny replied. 'Though I suppose it might just as easily be their son — perhaps he has a family by now?

'When Dan and Paul were boys, they were friends with Kit, until the family moved to London.'

'I think I might recognise Kit, even after all this time,' Sally said.

Jenny considered for a moment.

'I'm not sure I would,' she said.

The two friends negotiated a muddy path, and took the other way back to the village, via the winding road.

'I didn't see Gary at Will's shop this

morning,' Sally said as they fell into step once more.

'He's got an interview in Newquay today,' Jenny told her. 'Something to do with that river and shore project he's been on . . . conservation and stuff. Kerensa went along for moral support — and a day out.'

'Your son's nothing if not a tryer.'

'They've taken Ben. I hope my grandson behaves himself. Gary was so worried about this interview, and it won't help if Ben's being mischievous,' Jenny said.

'I'll keep my fingers crossed for them,' Sally promised.

'All four of them,' Jenny added. 'Now there's going to be another baby in the family!'

She chuckled, remembering her little grandson's face when he'd realised he was going to be a big brother.

'Ben told me he wants the baby to be a boy,' Jenny went on. 'He's somehow got it into his head a girl wouldn't know how to make proper sandcastles!'

It Was Fine!

Gary Hawke stepped out on to the busy Newquay pavement. He looked around anxiously, and then caught sight of Kerensa and Ben waiting for him hand-in-hand on the other side of the road. Thank goodness his interview was over now. There was nothing more he could do.

The tension in his shoulders eased as he smiled and waved. Ben waved back, bouncing on his toes as if fastened to a piece of elastic.

In another moment, Gary was beside them, ruffling Ben's hair and hugging Kerensa close.

'How was it?' his wife asked.

'The interview was fine,' Gary answered.

Kerensa's eyes brightened.

'So you've got the job?'

'I'm sorry, love. They said they'd be in touch.'

'I really want to know that we can move out of the Chough before this new baby arrives.' Kerensa sighed.

'That's another six months. A lot can happen in that time,' Gary said.

Kerensa nodded doubtfully.

'I want us to have our own place as much as you do,' he reassured her, kissing her cheek. 'But we'll have to be patient.'

The family linked hands. Ben hopped along the pavement between his parents.

'I'm afraid it's harder on you, at Mum's café all day with Ben, but there were lots of applicants at this interview,' Gary continued. 'I still have as good a chance as any.'

He spoke cheerfully, though Gary couldn't be sure he'd eventually get the job. Still, it wouldn't help Kerensa if he was gloomy about his prospects. And the interviewer had told him his practical experience around Penarren cove would be very much in his favour.

'I'll keep looking for other work, too,' Gary added.

'If there is any,' Kerensa said, looking uncharacteristically glum.

'I've still got my job with Will Gulliver, as well as the river conservation project. I'm one of the lucky ones, don't forget — '

'Look!' Ben shouted, tugging Gary's arm and pointing. 'Hot dog man!'

Gary looked at Kerensa and grinned.

'I think we all deserve one of those!' he said.

They sat on a wooden bench to eat. Ben wriggled between his parents. At last, the food claimed the little boy's full attention, and he concentrated on demolishing his hot dog while the adults watched the distant waves rolling over the rocks. The wind whipped Kerensa's dark curls across her face, and coloured her cheeks.

We Can't All Be Leaders

'It's like a holiday just to be away from the café!' Kerensa declared.

'You do get on all right with Mum these days, don't you?' Gary asked thoughtfully. 'I haven't heard you two have words in a long time.'

Kerensa nodded slowly.

'Mind you, there are still times when we don't see eye to eye,' she admitted. 'She's that determined, your mum. Won't listen to me, Lily, or anybody sometimes!'

Gary nodded sympathetically. He knew his mum tried to do too much, and sometimes expected the same of the rest of the family.

'I think Mum forgets that we don't see the café as our future. I understand why the Chough's important to her. It was my dad's place, after all, and he put so much of himself into it.

'Granfer's just as bad, these days, with his 'this needs a coat of paint' or 'I'll get up the ladder and put that right!' Neither he nor Mum can bear to think of the Chough fading away.'

'It must have been hard for her when your dad died,' Kerensa said.

'He was something of a hero around here, was my dad,' Gary said levelly.

'He was a very difficult act to follow . . . ' Kerensa looked thoughtfully at her husband. 'But we're not all cut out to be leaders in this life, are we?'

'I know I'm not,' Gary agreed. 'Well, not in the way my dad was, that's for sure.

'Plus . . . I'd really like to think our Ben would grow up feeling able to please the adults around him most of the time. Not like me, always worried in case I didn't get things right.'

'I'm sure your dad loved you, Gary . . . '

'We had some great times together, it's true. But there were rough patches.

My dad didn't really know how to deal with anyone who preferred studying plants and animals to tackling the next difficult cliff.'

'You know, I reckon you're just as determined as he was, in your own way.'

Gary looked fondly at his wife.

'You should know,' he said with a grin. 'I persuaded you to marry me!'

'Well, someone had to be the lucky girl,' Kerensa teased, rolling her blue eyes. 'Come on, we must get back. Being pregnant makes me hungry. I need my proper dinner.'

Unexpected Meeting

There ought to be some easier way of fastening wriggling children into safety seats, Gary thought as, finally, he heard Ben's harness click into place.

He let out a long breath as he turned the car on to the coast road. The sweep of the sea rolling into Watergate Bay calmed him.

He smiled at Kerensa, and saw she was frowning slightly.

'We'll be just in time to help with the lunchtime rush,' she said without enthusiasm.

'We can stop at Mawgan, if you like. Get ourselves a proper meal,' Gary offered.

Kerensa shook her head.

'The Chough's sure to have been busy. I don't want anyone to think I'm slacking.'

'I'm sure nobody would mind if you

put your feet up this afternoon,' Gary said.

'Lily's covering for me till I get back, but it wouldn't be fair to ask her to stay. She's got her other job at the Merrymaid this evening, when the sing-song starts.'

'Lily Pinch is another one who never stops,' Gary observed. 'Sometimes, I wish I could persuade certain folk to ease up. Take more time to appreciate life and stuff. Granfer, Mum, you . . . you're always on the go.'

'Not to mention Ben!' Kerensa said, laughing.

'Ben most of all!' Gary agreed. 'But he's been a good boy today, haven't you, Ben?'

He glanced in the driving mirror.

'Amazing. Our son's asleep,' Gary said.

'I'm not surprised — he's been running me off my feet since six o'clock this morning!' Kerensa said.

★　★　★

Gary put the car into a lower gear before starting down the narrow, twisty route into Penarren. As the blue-grey line of the sea reappeared on the horizon, he noticed a car to his right, parked at an unexpected angle. At the same moment, a tall figure stepped into the road.

With no time to brake, Gary swerved, squealing to a halt just short of the pathway leading from the farm.

'This is a bad junction!' he muttered fiercely, hauling up the handbrake with a shudder. The engine stalled. 'Thank goodness for safety belts.

'Kerensa?'

'We're OK,' she said, quickly checking her son. Ben's eyes had opened briefly, but he was asleep again already.

Gary looked back. The pedestrian he'd so nearly hit was striding towards them. Gary got out and leaned against his car, braced for strong words.

The tall, fair-haired man reached him quickly.

'I'm so sorry!' he said.

Gary was taken aback.

'No need to apologise. I was at least as much to blame.'

'Even so, I should have been more careful.'

'Well, let's just say we'll both take more care,' Gary said. 'This is a tricky turn if you're new around here.'

'I can hardly claim to be a newcomer. I was brought up at Trenfos,' the man said.

Somewhere in his mind, Gary felt information fall into place.

'You must be Mr Venning!' he said.

'Kit,' the man said firmly, holding out his hand.

Gary shook it.

'As long as everyone in your car is all right . . . ' Kit said.

'Is yours out of action? Do you need a lift anywhere?' Gary asked, worrying in case Kit Venning was more shaken than he appeared.

'I'd decided to walk,' he replied. 'I'm only going to the Merrymaid. I've heard they do live music. If you're going, perhaps we'll meet less abruptly this evening.'

'We might,' Gary called after him. 'I'm one of the singers.'

Gary climbed back into the car and restarted the engine.

'Who was that?' Kerensa asked.

'One of the long-lost Vennings, apparently. Not sure which, though. He's tall for his height, isn't he?' Gary joked, watching Kit stride away.

'Friendly, too, considering you nearly ran him over!' Kerensa teased.

Music At The Merrymaid

Jenny led the way from the windy pavement into the warmth and light of the main bar at the Merrymaid Inn. Someone was tuning a fiddle, someone else tried scales on an accordion, and yet another practised rhythms on a crowdy crawn, the large, handheld drum essential for Cornish folk tunes.

The landlord, Fred Trudgian, had lit the fire, for the evenings were still cool, and the reek of smoke mingled with the savoury tang of vinegar and hot chips.

'Oh, Lily's cooking smells good. I could do with something to eat,' Sally said. 'Shall we sit at this table, Jen?'

'Hi, Sal — and Jenny, my little sweetheart!' A figure loomed beside them. 'I've missed you! We must make a proper date again soon.'

Jenny had no time to respond before Paul's arms encircled her, and she felt the roughness of his navy sweater against her cheek.

'I've got a surprise for you!' Paul said, beaming as he set Jenny back on her feet.

'What's that?' she asked, getting her breath back.

For answer, Paul waved to a figure already chatting with a group of Penarreners in the centre of the room. The man smiled and came over.

'It's a who, not a what,' Paul said enigmatically. He drew the man forward. 'Kit, you must remember Jenny Hawke. Her dad was Coxswain Trelawney of the *Etta* not so long ago'.

'Hello,' Paul's companion said, grinning. 'I'm on a mission this evening to discover exactly how many folk can remember who I am after so long away!'

Jenny shook the hand Kit offered, doing her best to match her memory of her husband's shy boyhood friend with the smiling, confident man in front of her.

'Of course. Kit Venning! Dan often spoke of you . . . How are you finding life in Penarren, now you're back?' Jenny said.

'Believe me, it's good to be home!' Kit said warmly.

He took the offered seat between Jenny and her father. Paul and Sally sat opposite.

'Are you back at Trenfos for good?' Garron asked.

Kit wriggled one hand in a gesture of uncertainty.

'It depends,' he said. 'I really hope so.'

He turned to address Jenny.

'I hope you don't mind, Jenny, but I must tell you how sorry I was to hear of Dan's death. He was such a power-house. I'm sure you know what a good friend he was to me when we were young. It must have been very hard for you when it happened.'

'I had my dad, and Gary, thank goodness,' Jenny said. 'You can't give up when a child depends on you.'

'I was living in London when I heard.

Work and noise seemed never-ending then. It really brought home to me everything I missed about Penarren,' Kit replied.

'If I lived in London these days,' Sally put in, 'it wouldn't be hard to persuade me to leave!'

'At least my work meant I was travelling around for part of the time,' Kit continued. 'But it made sense to keep a base in the capital. It's less important these days, and anyway, when my father died I was determined to live in Penarren again some day.'

'Is your own family with you?' Paul asked.

Kit smiled, and drew a photograph from his wallet.

'If I can persuade her!' he said. 'This is my daughter, Beatrice.'

Jenny glimpsed a slender girl in a red dress, her long, blonde hair swept by the wind. She was striking a model pose and laughing.

'She's lovely,' Jenny said. 'How old is she?'

'Eighteen, going on thirty-five,' Kit said ruefully, 'Or thirteen! It depends on her mood.'

'Teenagers!' Jenny sympathised, meeting Kit's green eyes with a smile. 'We've been there, too.

'Will your wife and daughter travel here soon?'

'Melissa and I are divorced,' Kit said. He fidgeted with a beer mat on the table. 'Amicably, as they say . . . '

'I'm sorry,' Jenny said. She had a sudden vision of him alone in the empty house at Trenfos, and felt sad. 'But you must both be proud of your daughter?'

'One thing her mother and I do agree on,' Kit confirmed, gazing at the photograph. Jenny was pleased to see he meant it.

'I'm sure she'll love Penarren as much as you do,' she said.

'It's great to be back, but I wish I'd kept up better with my Penarren friends — ' Kit said.

'Dan was never the sort to write

letters, either,' Jenny reassured him. 'Still, you're here now. Be warned — everyone will want to know your deepest secrets, but then, as a Penarr-ener born, you should know what to expect!'

Kit chuckled.

'Lily Pinch has already invited me to tea. I'm preparing to be grilled along with the toasted tea-cakes!'

'You're a lucky man,' Paul said, leaning across. 'Lily's Cornish fairings are the best, but you'd know that — didn't Lily work for your parents in the old days?'

Kit nodded.

'She often helped out when I was a child . . . when my mother was ill. Her baking's definitely one of the reasons I came back!'

Jenny had no time to wonder exactly what Kit's other reasons might be, because at that moment a chair was tapped, and a chord struck. The first notes sounded light, almost casual, but then the music gained volume and a beat, and a familiar tune emerged.

'The Song Of The Western Men' was a favourite with them all, so it wasn't long before everyone joined the chorus. Jenny exchanged a smile with Sally as they heard Paul Biddick's voice roar above the rest. No Trelawney was going to die while Paul had anything to say about it! He was, as ever, determinedly off-key, but Jenny and Sally had long agreed sing-along evenings wouldn't be the same without him.

'That was great!' Paul said to a smiling Garron as the last notes died away.

'Now I really know I'm back!' Kit added, joining the applause.

Jenny felt someone else sink into the seat beside her, and turned to pat her son's arm. He must be tired after the interview.

'I didn't think you'd be coming,' she said.

'I couldn't let the lads down,' Gary said. 'I promised to give them a song.'

'Where's Kerensa?'

'We had a babysitter lined up, but she was so tired after we got Ben to bed, I persuaded her to stay put and rest.'

Jenny introduced her son to Kit.

'Good to meet you properly,' Kit said with a grin, shaking Gary's hand. 'But, forgive me, I hadn't realised you were Dan Hawke's son. I remember your dad well.'

Jenny was fascinated by the way Kit coaxed Gary into conversation. She knew how reserved her son could be, and yet he was soon chatting to Kit like an old friend.

Making a Difference

'What plans do you have, now you're back?' Gary asked.

Kit rubbed his face thoughtfully.

'Quite a few,' he said, smiling.

'If you're here to splash some London money about, there's always the lifeboat fund!' Sally put in, only half joking.

'I owe Penarren such a lot,' Kit said. 'I came back with the idea of making a difference, if I can.'

'Maybe folk will take you more seriously when you've got something down on paper.' Garron tapped the table with his broad forefinger. 'You should know we Cornish don't like pie-in-the-sky talk!'

Kit twisted in his seat to face Jenny's father.

'In fact, I've submitted provisional plans, Mr Trelawney. I'd be delighted if people wanted to look them over. Especially retired coxswains!'

'You're on, my handsome!' Garron said, clapping Kit on the shoulder.

★   ★   ★

The fiddles and drum began again, slower than before.

'Where's that Gary Hawke?' one of the musicians called. 'He do know this song well . . . '

Gary stood up.

'Come on then, me 'andsome!' the drummer said, waving him forward. 'And just quiet down, you noisy rabble at the back! This is a romantic one . . . '

Jenny's son had a good, strong tenor voice and a great love and understanding of the songs he sang.

Jenny listened as Gary sang the familiar lyrics of 'The Water Is Wide', thinking, as she often did, of his late father.

Dan Hawke had clambered joyfully through life fearing nothing, and seemingly unaware that not everyone shared his intrepid spirit. She touched Dan's long-ago gift, the silver bracelet around her wrist.

She knew he and his son had had their differences while Gary was growing up, but without a constant stream of fresh challenges to master, Dan simply would not have been the man she loved.

If they'd been blessed with more time together, she knew Gary would have come to understand him, too. He and Dan had shared the same determination, if not the same interests.

Gary's song ended and he regained his seat to appreciative clapping.

'That was lovely,' Jenny said as one of the fiddlers struck up a solo jig.

'Thanks,' Gary said, relaxing and sipping his drink. 'I'll take myself off home as soon as I've finished this, Mum.' He yawned. 'It's been quite a day!'

Gone To Bodmin

'Have you taken enough bread out of the freezer, Kerensa?' Jenny called to her daughter-in-law as they worked busily behind the counter at the Chough the following afternoon. 'We're going to need plenty of sandwiches for teatime.'

Kerensa, washing up the last of the lunchtime plates in the café kitchen, dried her hands.

'I'll get started as soon as I've put this lot away,' she said.

'Thanks,' Jenny said, bustling past. 'Best to be prepared.'

'What about cakes?' Kerensa asked over her shoulder.

'I've just popped some plain sponges in the oven,' Jenny said. 'I'll ask Dad to get them out once the timer pings . . . '

Kerensa stopped stacking and glanced at her mother-in-law.

'Granfer's out,' she said.

'Out?'

'Out, as in 'gone to Bodmin'. He said he'd told you.'

Jenny pushed at her fringe, annoyed with herself as much as her father. She'd heard recently that forgetfulness could be caused by having too much to remember; she could well believe it. She remembered now: Garron had let her know he was going out, but with so many other events crowding her mind, she had completely forgotten.

'Did he say what time he'd be back?' she asked.

'Not to me.' Kerensa shrugged.

'Funny, I'm sure Dad never mentioned going as far as Bodmin this morning,' Jenny murmured, half to herself.

She glanced up to see Paul opening the café door, and called Kerensa to help at the counter as quickly as she could. While her daughter-in-law served at one end, Jenny stood at the other.

Paul held the door wide for a family

of four visitors then ushered Kit in behind them.

'Hi, Jenny!' he called, catching a smiling Kit on the shoulder. 'Got you another customer. Not that you need promoting today by the looks of things!'

'Everyone's welcome,' Jenny said, setting out plates. 'What'll you have?'

'We're a bit late for lunch, but I told Kit this was the place for proper pasties,' Paul said.

'One thing I can claim is that I never forgot the famous Penarren Chough pasty!' Kit protested, leaning on the counter.

A timer buzzed in the kitchen.

'I hope you don't mind waiting half a minute,' Jenny said, trying not to feel flustered. 'I have to see to some baking.'

A Gifted Singer

As she pushed at the double doors Jenny felt, not for the first time, that she ought to organise extra help for busy occasions like these. If only her dad hadn't taken it into his head to go traipsing off today!

She set the sponges to cool and hurried back.

'Sorry,' she said. ' 'Pasties, was it? How many?'

'One, please,' Kit said.

'Two for me,' Paul said with a wink. 'I'm a growing lad, you know!'

Jenny laughed and lifted another on to a hot plate.

'I'll bet even you can't manage two Chough pasties at one go, Pauley Biddick,' she said. 'But if you want the second wrapped to take away, I can do that for you!'

She waved a hand towards the end of the counter.

'Some people think it spoils the taste, but there's tomato sauce if you'd like some, Kit.'

'I wouldn't dream of it. These are a meal in themselves.' Kit paused while Jenny served their steaming pasties.

'Did you enjoy yourself yesterday evening?' he asked with a smile.

'Nothing like a good sing-song, is there?' Jenny said.

'Your son is a gifted singer,' Kit observed. 'He reminded me of his father — '

'Danny couldn't sing,' Paul interrupted him. 'Any more'n I can! They used to say at school we were the two that growled in the Key of Biddick.'

Kit shook his head.

'I didn't mean that, so much. I meant . . . somehow his attitude was similar. Dan was always able to sum people up, and Gary got to the heart of his song in a similar way.

'Sorry, I'm not putting this very well . . . '

'Not at all,' Jenny said quietly. 'I feel the same when I hear Gary sing.'

Jenny thought Kit wanted to say more, but at that moment Paul tried to pick up his second pasty. He whistled sharply and blew on his heated fingers.

'There now! You know how hot they are,' Jenny scolded.

'You're telling me!' Paul winced.

'Put your fingers in cold water,' Kit suggested.

Paul shook his head. Instead, he waved his hand around a few times, and then reached across the counter to capture Jenny's.

'I know how to take my mind off the pain!' he said. 'I'll ask Jenny for a date. Where would you like us to go, sweetheart?'

'Anywhere calm and stress-busting,' Jenny said with feeling.

'I was meaning to ask where people go to relax these days,' Kit said, settling himself at a table. 'Apart from the Merrymaid or the beach, of course.'

'We sometimes see a film in Newquay,' Jenny said. 'Perhaps you'd like to come? We could ask Sally, too.'

She saw Paul pull a quick face.

'Aren't you and Sal friends at the moment, Paul?' she murmured.

'I'm not in her good books, just now,' he admitted. 'I tipped a drink over her skirt last night. Accidental, it was. I said I'd wash it, but she told me I'd only make it worse. She did go on a bit.'

Jenny grinned.

'Sally never stays cross with you for long,' she said. 'Take a risk, and ask her.'

'She can only say no,' Kit said.

'Are you coming with us?' Paul asked Kit.

'If you're sure I wouldn't be intruding.' Kit smiled.

'Not at all. It's only our usual friendly outing,' Jenny said, smiling back as she wiped the counter. 'It would be nice for us all to go together.'

*   *   *

'Kerensa's taken an order of cakes to Gulliver's. I didn't know Dad would be out this long.' Jenny bustled into the back room after closing the café. 'I'm really grateful you could take care of Ben, Lily. Will you stay for tea?'

'That'd be lovely,' Lily Pinch said from Jenny's settee.

Ben happily chugged a toy car around Lily's feet.

'What's your dad up to?' Lily called as Jenny clattered plates in the small family kitchen.

'I'm not sure,' Jenny called back. She paused, waiting for the kettle to boil. Looking out, she became pleasantly distracted by the view towards the tidal creek.

In summer, her window framed a perfect watercolour, complete with soft greenery, washed pebbles and a flurry of small ducks. Jenny knew nowhere with quite this contrast of rough sea and sweet, sheltered waters.

The kettle boiled.

Everyone was settled at the table a few minutes later when the front door opened. Garron came straight in. Gary and Kerensa followed close behind.

'I saw Ted Berryman, over at the

planning office,' Garron began, not waiting for questions.

'Who?' Jenny asked.

'I helped save his life once on the *Etta*,' Garron said. 'Not that we mentioned it, of course. But he said he'd never forget me, and he didn't. He copied these.'

Jenny's father spread a crackling paper on the table, carefully avoiding Ben's plate of baked beans.

They all gathered round and peered at the plans.

Clearly marked, the Chough sat, as ever, beside the river with its face to the sea. Two new boundaries were marked nearby.

'These are provisional plans submitted by Mr Kitto Venning and company for small shops and a children's play area,' Garron said. 'I'm not sure I like them.'

'I think we could do with some extra interest here,' Jenny said. 'Besides, Kit seemed very open and friendly about it last night.'

Garron's Warning

Garron jabbed angrily at the map.

'Can't you see?' he demanded. 'It'll affect the river! Penarren's going to lose any claim to being a quiet haven once this gets going!'

'I hope they'll consult properly about wildlife.' Gary sounded anxious.

'All your work from the last couple of years could be wiped out at a stroke!' Garron asserted.

'That's a bit dramatic, surely?' Jenny was thoughtful. 'Look, the main changes will be nearer the harbour . . . '

She traced her finger across the map, coming to a halt beside the lifeboat station.

'You might start seeing things differently if this means your own son will lose his job,' Garron said.

'I can't believe that anyone Penarren-born would do anything to ruin one of our main attractions, Dad!'

'Just because he was an old friend of Dan's doesn't mean he'll get everything right, Jenny. And there's something else. Your ideas for reopening the river terrace — Penarren folks' reactions might be one difficulty . . . but what if you clash with Kit directly?'

Jenny hesitated, and the delicate watercolour scene from her window came to mind. She blinked it away, certain her dad was overreacting.

'All the more reason to co-operate. Make sure our views are taken into account from the beginning.'

Garron folded his arms.

'You obviously don't remember what the Vennings were like, do you? But I'm telling you, I do — only too well!'

I'm Counting On You

'I'm calling a meeting about Kit Venning's plans for Penarren,' Jenny's father said, adjusting his peaked blue cap to show he meant business. 'Sooner rather than later!'

'There are lots of folk who would come to support Coxswain Trelawney,' Jenny said thoughtfully, wrapping another batch of lunchtime sandwiches. 'But won't you need all shades of opinion working together if we're going to get anywhere?'

'You're right, Jenny,' Garron said. 'We should make a proper job of it. Show everyone around here how important this could be for the future of the village, especially with the summer season coming up.

'We'll get busy with advertising. Invite the Press, a couple of photographers, our local councillor.'

'What about Kit Venning and his team?' Jenny asked quietly.

Garron acknowledged this with a brief nod.

'This meeting will be open to all!' he declared.

Jenny was relieved. Garron might act tough, but she knew he'd want the meeting to be fair.

The rattle of bread crates being stacked outside the Chough interrupted their conversation. Garron pulled his cap further forward and made for the door.

'I want you there, Jenny!' he called over his shoulder. 'I'm counting on you to represent our interests.'

'I'll be there,' Jenny promised.

She heard her father outside, bantering good-naturedly with the bread man. Sighing, she pulled another roll of sandwich wrap across the counter. She realised she had yet to define the Chough's interests, even to herself.

She and Garron seldom agreed on anything, at first. But this issue was too important for them to appear divided in public. Jenny sighed again, and hoped she was worrying unnecessarily about that meeting.

The Community Gathers

With Garron in such a forceful mood, the evening was soon arranged. The following week, Jenny found herself climbing the steep road up towards St Piran's church and the village hall, still troubled by thoughts of division. Perhaps everyone would end the meeting in harmony, but she had to admit it was doubtful.

She pushed at the studded wooden door and found the hall full of chairs, talk and people. Following the clink of china and the aroma of hot coffee and sweet biscuits, Jenny made her way through the throng of villagers to the back of the hall.

She looked towards the platform, where Garron and Kit sat on brown plastic chairs, smiling gamely for a photograph. A flash lit the scene as a reporter recorded them for the local paper.

A friendly figure offered Jenny a Cornish fairing. Her mind was so full she nearly forgot to murmur her thanks to Paul's mum, Morwenna Biddick, as she accepted the biscuit with her coffee.

'Thank you for coming, ladies and gentlemen!' Garron announced.

It looked to Jenny as though her father was surveying the gathering exactly as if he were still on the bridge of the lifeboat, the *Etta Trelawney*.

'Are we all ready . . . ?'

The former coxswain's steady voice rang out, and Jenny couldn't help feeling proud. She knew her dad missed those times when he was clearly in charge, but tonight he was in his element once more.

Jenny slid along a row of chairs and found a seat next to Sally Rosewarne.

'Hi,' Sally whispered. 'Who's the girl sitting beside Kit?'

Jenny shook her head.

'I don't think it's his daughter,' she murmured. 'Must be an assistant.'

The reporter searched for a seat in

the front row, and Garron waited courteously until she'd found one.

'As you know,' Jenny's father continued, 'we're here about the proposals for our village. I think we all felt some sort of discussion was in order.'

'Better 'n all them rumours flying about!' Fred Trudgian, the landlord of the Merrymaid Inn, grumbled.

Jenny heard a swell of agreement around him.

'Luckily we have the very person here tonight to answer your questions,' Garron said firmly. 'I'm sure you all know young Mr Venning who's recently returned to Penarren . . .

'Kit, would you like to launch our meeting down the slipway?'

Kit acknowledged Garron's introduction with a smile and unfolded his tall frame from his seat on the platform.

'I think we all know how important tourism is to our livelihood here,' Kit said. 'As a Cornishman, I know for certain that Penarren lies on the most beautiful coastline in the country. But we're tucked away here and we're still not an obvious place for people to visit. I've proposed some relatively small changes that will help to put Penarren on the map.'

'What do you mean by 'small'?' someone asked.

'I'll speak about each area in turn, if that's OK. First, improved access to the beach.'

'We always need more car parking!' another villager piped up. 'We get proper jammed up sometimes!'

Kit nodded.

'That's one thing we agree on,' he said. 'I don't know about you, but I feel that having cars spilling on to farmers' fields is a nuisance for everyone.'

Again, there were nods of agreement.

Kit cleared his throat.

'I'd also like to suggest a grant to update — or perhaps rescue would be a better word — some of the existing tumble-down buildings near the harbour.'

'You'll have your work cut out!' Fred

shouted. 'They're Ancient Monuments, more like!'

'No — go on! Put those eyesores to good use!' Fred's neighbour called.

Kit smiled.

'They could be rented and used as craft stalls, small display galleries or information centres, for instance,' he continued. 'I'm glad we agree that's another thing that's not only possible, but desirable.'

A Village Divided

Jenny saw nodding heads all around her. Was Penarren really going to support proposals for change, after all? Her attention was arrested by the set look on Mrs Biddick's face. Clearly Morwenna wasn't in favour, no matter what the general feeling of the meeting might be.

Kit glanced in Jenny's direction and smiled.

'There's another scheme, which I have to admit is close to my heart,' he said. 'I'm proposing a children's area, which I hope can be developed somewhere between the Chough and the point where the coastal path crosses the river.'

There was silence for a moment.

'You can't put swings and round-abouts and . . . and *tarmac* and stuff, alongside of the creek!'

Jenny was shocked to recognise her son's voice. He was standing just inside the door. She hadn't realised Gary had followed her to the meeting, let alone that he would ever speak up so vehemently in public.

Garron made as if to call his grandson to order, but Kit gestured to reassure him that he had no objection to Gary's outburst.

'It doesn't have to mean swings on metal frames, Gary. The details can be sorted out once we agree in principle. At present we're only here to discuss what's best — '

Morwenna Biddick could contain herself no longer.

'Building by the creek won't be the bettermost thing you'm ever thought of, young Kitto, mark my words. You tell 'un, Coxswain Trelawney! After all, 'tis your daughter's business that's going to be affected by new goings-on that side of the village.'

Garron frowned and shuffled awkwardly in his seat.

'You know as well as I do, Morwenna Biddick, that the chairman of this meeting must remain neutral. But we're all here to have our say, and I'm sure Jenny can speak for herself.'

As her father nodded towards her, Jenny had the unnerving experience of being watched by the entire meeting. Everyone seemed to be waiting for her to support her son and Morwenna. But that wasn't going to be so easy . . .

'I'd certainly want to know the details before giving my wholehearted support,' she said cautiously. 'But I believe in thinking positively, and attracting new visitors in the direction of the Chough seems an excellent idea to me.'

Morwenna tut-tutted loudly.

Jenny tried to gauge the reactions in the faces along the platform. She had the oddest feeling that Kit was suppressing his surprise at her response. Garron, she saw, was still frowning. Gary was behind her.

Jenny didn't turn to see her son's

reaction, but she guessed it wouldn't be long before he let her know what he thought at home.

Penarren opinion was splitting like a wooden log. In her heart Jenny feared she'd just swung another blow of the axe.

Family Fallout

'What did you make of last night's meeting, Granfer?' Gary asked, helping Ben pour milk on his breakfast cereal.

Garron took a sip of scalding tea. He was paying greater attention to his daughter than to the mug in his hand.

Jenny was still in her dressing-gown. She was gazing at the creek from the kitchen window and her restless fingers were tapping the counter.

'It would have taken some sort of miracle for us all to agree straightaway, I suppose,' Garron said at last.

'But do you really think anything — even a children's playground — could be built on that site and not cause problems for the wildlife?' Gary demanded.

'Maybe,' Garron said neutrally. Inwardly,

he had the same misgivings as his grandson.

'It only takes small changes to any habitat and . . . whoosh!' Gary swept one hand through the air. 'In just one season all the good work done in the last few years is wiped out for good!'

'I know,' Garron said. He realised he was waiting for his daughter to join this conversation. Her silence was making him uneasy.

'What do you think, Jenny?' he asked eventually.

Jenny, still gazing through the window, shook her head.

'I don't know . . . ' she began. She turned to face them. 'Well . . . yes, I do. The problem is what I said last night — detail. I understand Gary's feelings, but we still don't know for sure what will be built there. And surely we'll be entitled to have our say before anything is made final . . . ?'

'But, Mum!' Gary interrupted. 'You know as well as I do, it only takes a couple of blokes charging in with their diggers and lorries to churn everything into mud . . . '

'Only if it's tackled the wrong way, Gary!'

Gary's face hardened in disagreement.

Jenny turned back to the window.

'I'd be as sorry as anyone to sacrifice this view down to the cove,' she said. 'But neither the Chough nor Penarren can afford to stand still. Speaking of which . . . it's high time I was dressed . . . '

The kitchen became a whirl of activity as Garron moved aside to let his daughter hurry upstairs and Kerensa rushed in to wash Ben before playgroup.

'I'd better be off to work,' Gary said.

'Say cheerio to Daddy,' Kerensa told Ben, accepting a kiss from Gary as she hurried out the door.

'Byeee.' Ben waved.

The family bustle at the Chough over for another morning, Gary paused in the doorway.

'What have you got planned today, Granfer?' he asked.

'I'll maybe go for a walkabout,' Garron said, draining his mug. 'Down along the creek.'

A Precious Haven

Garron Trelawney knew Penarren as well as he knew his own square hands. As a boy, he'd floated dry reeds and paper boats in the stream that bubbled down the valley. It ran past the Chough, gradually widening towards the cove. At low tide it wandered in shining ribbons through the wetted sand until it reached the sea.

Garron stopped and looked to his left where the Chough's sign swung gently in the sea breeze. Around his feet there was a tough tangle of grasses and creeping willow, growing greener and more lush nearer the stream. He pushed at the earth, making crescent shapes with his toe, trying to imagine how things might change.

He knelt to scoop the rough soil and weighed it in his hand. He thought of the Chough, and of his daughter's struggles after Dan had been killed. Together, they'd held on and kept her business running.

Garron swallowed. They had invested so much more than money in that old café. He battled the intense feelings that surged within him. Coxswains, even retired coxswains, had to stay strong, no matter what.

But he couldn't help feeling that attracting more tourist families to this peaceful spot might not be good for the Chough or the environment.

A children's area would need secure fencing. Fixing posts and laying surfaces would mean bringing in building materials. Not only would that mean traffic, where no traffic had been seen before, but what would all those hard surfaces mean for the plants and animals already here?

Garron let the earth trickle through his fingers for a few moments. Then he brushed his hands and set off purposefully around the cove in the direction of the lifeboat station. The former coxswain knew he was always welcome there, and right now he needed the *Etta*'s uncomplicated company.

Old Friends

Paul Biddick, a polishing rag in his hand, appeared deep in thought beside the gleaming lifeboat.

'Thought I'd find you here, Pauley,' Garron greeted him.

'Want some news?' Paul looked up with a quick smile.

'What's that, then?' The former coxswain reached out his right hand and laid it on the *Etta*'s rail, taking heart from the contact with his old friend.

'Kit Venning's been asking when he can apply for training,' Paul continued. 'He wants to join the crew!'

'Does he now?' Garron smiled, too, though he was unable to summon up his usual warmth. There hadn't been a Venning on the strength for a long time. Still, the training would sort things out.

'And . . . ' Paul paused for dramatic

effect ' . . . he wants to put some of the latest communications equipment our way. Global Positioning System. No expense spared, seemingly.'

Garron's eyebrows shot up.

'Does he know how much — ?' he asked.

Paul nodded.

'One thing about our Kitto. He takes care he's well clued-up before he starts,' Paul said. 'So I reckon we can take it he do know exactly how much he's talking about.'

'Even so . . . ' Garron mused. 'That's very generous. The fundraising committee will be well pleased.'

'I don't deny it would be money well spent,' Paul said, taking a clean duster to polish an already gleaming rail. 'But some people won't see it that way.'

'The returned exile buying his way back into the community?' Garron wondered aloud. 'Yes, I'm afraid I'd thought of that, too, but I didn't want to sound ungrateful.'

Thoughtfully, Garron stood back.

The lifeboat had been, and still was, his joy. Over the years they'd all known both triumph and tragedy in her. He felt his retirement as coxswain almost as a bereavement, missing daily the roll of the deck beneath his feet. He'd forced himself to be content with his new rôle as the *Etta*'s greatest fundraiser and land support, but his interest in her future on the sea would not abate.

Garron Trelawney found his mind caught in a rare flight of fancy. He pictured a fully trained Kit Venning, in the familiar orange suit of the lifeboatman, gripping the wet handrail of the *Etta* as the waves crashed around him. A new generation of the *Etta*'s crew — Garron felt a sudden chill, as if his past had begun to slip away from him. Would he still be as much a part of the *Etta*'s extended family in times to come?

Busy Afternoon

'We weren't exactly run off our feet this morning, Dad,' Jenny said on her father's return to the Chough. 'But I'm glad you're back!'

'Promised I'd help out this afternoon, didn't I?' Garron said, carefully placing his peaked cap on a hook in the hall. 'Why don't you take some time off — you've been working flat out recently. How about a nice walk?'

Jenny rolled her apron behind the counter and counted off her errands on her fingers.

'First I have to take some of our Chough biscuits to Will Gulliver's shop. Next, I need to catch the library van. I have to nip to the post office to buy some stamps, too. Then it's off to Lily Pinch's for a cuppa.'

Jenny paused for breath.

'After that, if there's time, I might

take that walk along the cliff path!'

She gave her dad a swift hug as they passed each other, then pulled on her battered anorak.

'Kerensa and Ben will be back from playgroup any minute,' she called over her shoulder on the way out. 'I've done some tomato soup for Ben's lunch. The sandwiches are in the fridge and there's fresh fruit on the counter — '

Spotting Garron shaking his head at her sad inability to leave any of the Chough's organisation to him, Jenny stopped. Smiling ruefully to herself, she headed off across Penarren square.

★   ★   ★

Later, wondering when she would get the time to enjoy the new library book nestling in her basket, Jenny made her way to Lily Pinch's grey-stone cottage, tucked away behind the main street.

'Tea's brewing,' Lily said comfortably, waving Jenny into her tiny living room. 'Sit down, and we'll have a bit o' gossip.'

Jenny settled herself into a cosy chair and relaxed.

'What did you make of last night's meeting, then?' Lily asked, bustling in with the tea-tray.

'It made me think,' Jenny admitted carefully.

Lily plumped a cushion. A feather flew.

'Kit Venning might not stay around to see things through. Has anybody thought of that?'

'Why wouldn't he?' Jenny asked. 'He's hardly a complete outsider.'

'Some settle, some don't. That be a fact, Jenny.'

Lily sank into an armchair that all but swallowed her small frame. Jenny couldn't help smiling at her friend's habitual no-nonsense expression.

'Kit told me his daughter might be coming to stay with him,' Jenny said. 'That doesn't sound to me like someone hurrying to move on.'

'I'm not saying he will go, Jenny. I'm just saying with that family it's best to be prepared for anything.'

'But you worked for the Vennings and you knew Kit as a child — what do you make of him now?' Jenny asked.

'He was such a quiet lad,' Lily remembered. She chuckled suddenly. 'He used to struggle, helping me mop. Swabbing decks, he called it. I wasn't surprised he'd asked about joining the *Etta* . . . '

'He has?' Jenny was intrigued. 'That has to be another reason in favour of him staying,' she said.

'There's something else I remember about our Kitto,' Lily went on, apparently wandering off the point. 'He was always wanting my help with those little building-brick models. But he needed watching.

'He had such imagination. He hardly ever lost his temper, but he had so many ideas, and if he couldn't get one to work, well — He wanted proof positive why something wasn't coming out right . . . he could never give up on anything once he'd started!'

Lily shifted comfortably in her seat.

'His father called him a stubborn cheel,' she went on, 'but truth to tell, old Mr Venning was a difficult so-and-so himself. Kit's not so much like his dad, but he must have learned something from him.'

'Kit must have been determined, not to say tough, to make such a success of his business in London,' Jenny mused. 'Running the Chough is small potatoes by comparison. I only hope he hasn't become the sort of person who's prepared to ride roughshod over the interests of lads like my Gary. He's put so much into his work here.'

'I suppose he might try,' Lily said. 'After all, business is business! But if he did, he could count on having the whole of Penarren against him, instead of just about half!'

'You sound as if you don't like our Mr Venning much, Lily.'

Lily shook her head.

'I always liked the lad. He can be very charming. But I can't say I favour his ideas.

'Will you have another cake, Jenny, dear? I made these from one of Morwenna Biddick's recipes. I must pass it on to you some time.'

Jenny accepted Lily's change of tack along with the cake, though she longed to ask more.

It seemed to her as though there were as many opinions of Kit as there were people to voice them, but they all appeared to be united on one thing. Even among his outright supporters, Kit's ideas made people uneasy.

Jenny sighed. As she kissed her friend goodbye, she found she was longing for that cliff walk.

A Breath of Fresh Air

There was a fresh wind blowing as Jenny climbed the cliff path towards Penarren Head. The unfolding view of sea, sky and white-topped waves was the one she loved above all. She'd come to sit on this rocky headland, where the pink thrift flowers clustered around her feet, in happy times and sad.

Dan always used to say that the outcrop high above the cove was an ancient chough gazing out to sea, and would claim that their café was named after it. Jenny didn't know if that was true, but she always felt this was a place where she could remember Dan happily.

There was someone else here today. Facing the waves with his collar turned up against the breeze, he was lost in thought. Not wanting to disturb him, she made to hurry past without speaking.

But then a voice called her name.

'Kit! What are you doing here?' Jenny exclaimed.

'Same as you, I imagine. Clearing my head.' He released his grip on his collar and put out a hand. 'Sorry, I didn't mean to make you jump!'

Jenny smiled and joined him.

'My head's full after a gossipy tea with Lily. What's your excuse?' she asked with a smile.

He gave a gentle shrug.

'I had news this morning.'

'Good?' Jenny asked him tentatively.

'Beatrice would like to visit her old dad . . . ' Kit said through tight lips.

'Aren't you pleased?'

'Yes, of course,' he said. 'But . . . '

Jenny looked at Kit carefully. His freckled face didn't seem accustomed to frowning, yet he looked worried.

'It's my ex-wife,' Kit went on.

Jenny thought he seemed relieved to be talking.

'She . . . Melissa's remarrying next month, and . . . '

'Oh . . . I see . . . '

'No upset there — at least, I don't think so. It's hard to tell, isn't it? Sorting out feelings, and so on. But, no, I'm sure that Melissa's marrying the right guy this time.'

'It's good that you can look at it like that.'

'I wish Beatrice felt the same! We've both explained everything to her as well as we could manage, but I think she always hoped we'd get back together.'

'Painful for her . . . ' Jenny said sympathetically.

'But my daughter's way of dealing with pain is never quiet. She seems to blame me for not rushing up to London to stop the wedding! I find it hard to sympathise when she insists on yelling at me down the phone every evening.'

'Often that's the only way youngsters believe they can show their feelings. She's growing up all the time — she'll soon be more able to cope.'

'I suppose the real trouble is, Jenny, it makes me feel so guilty about everything ... even about coming back to Penarren ...'

Penarren Magic

Kit gazed out over the cove. 'But maybe she'll benefit from the more peaceful atmosphere when she visits,' he said at last, hope sounding in his voice. 'Look at this place! The pink flowers all the way along the path. Those dark cliffs, and the caves where we used to play as kids. The harbour . . . the water slapping the little boats . . . the smell of salt and seaweed . . . '

'You think a bit of Penarren magic will do the trick?' Jenny suggested, feeling a smile tug at the corners of her mouth. 'I'd agree. It works every time, Kit. I bet your daughter will love it!'

'I've wanted to come home for so long,' Kit said, taking a deep breath. 'These changes . . . I've been seeing them in my mind for years. Now I can't help thinking how wonderful it would be to have

Beatrice here to watch them take shape!'

Caught by Kit's enthusiasm, Jenny found her own smile widening. His green eyes met hers and in that instant she knew, no matter what anyone said, that Penarren needed someone like Kit Venning.

'I'm sure there are plenty of people ready to give their support,' Jenny said. 'I don't think anyone doubts that the tourist industry in our little corner of the coast could do with a boost!'

'Thank you!' Kit said warmly. 'Do you know, Jenny, it's really helped to talk to you like this? It would be really valuable if a Penarren businesswoman could spare the time for more discussions.'

Jenny was more than happy to agree. Kit's obvious concern for his daughter's feelings had reassured her that he wasn't in the habit of riding roughshod over anyone. She hurried back to the Chough. She couldn't wait to share her new optimism with her father.

Jenny breezed back downhill, one

arm held across her waist to subdue the flapping of her old anorak in the breeze. She had a pang of regret that her attire made her look anything but business-like. To her amazement, she found she was actually contemplating dropping it in the dustbin when she got in. Maybe she would ask Sally to help her choose something smarter.

Council of War

Jenny let herself into the Chough kitchen through the back door, hoping to find her father. But he wasn't there. Instead, she heard an unfamiliar hubbub coming from the café's dining room. Garron's voice rose above the rest.

'I'm agreeing with you more and more, Morwenna Biddick!' Garron thundered. 'But the point is, how do we go about putting our point of view? Kit Venning's already worked out all the angles!'

The kitchen's double doors swished open. Gary, sporting a large linen apron tied around his middle, came in looking flustered.

'Good job Will Gulliver didn't need me to stay late,' he grumbled. 'Kerensa's been run off her feet.'

'Why?' Jenny asked. 'I thought Dad was minding the shop.'

Jenny's son ducked his head to indicate where his grandfather was sitting.

'Not any more,' he said. 'Granfer seems to be chairing a meeting.'

Jenny peered through the open door to see Garron presiding at a table-full of Penarreners.

Kerensa followed her husband into the kitchen, and leaned back against the wall, puffing a strand of hair off her hot face.

'They've finished the tea and cakes I gave them long ago,' she said. 'I don't want to drive away custom, Jenny, but they're causing quite an upset out there.'

'Upset?'

'Mrs Biddick and Fred Trudgian, plus a few others,' Gary informed her. 'They arrived about half an hour after you left — and before you could say 'redevelopment' they were sitting round that table in the corner, arguing the toss about who was going to tell Mr Venning they didn't like his plans, or his high-handed ways.'

'But he's not high-handed!' Jenny was dismayed. Opposition to the plans was one thing, but personal attack was quite another. 'He wants to talk.'

'Perhaps!' Gary said grimly.

Jenny felt trouble with a capital T pitching its tent between them. With a last glance at her son, she pushed at the doors and hurried through to the dining room.

She counted six people round the table, and she'd known every one of them all her life.

Morwenna, her husband Ben, and Fred Trudgian might have been expected to want things to be left as they were. But Paul was a younger generation. Did he really feel the same way about this as his parents? She had thought her friend would have thought and felt as she did. She was convinced Dan would have been in the forefront of any changes that might benefit Penarren.

Outsider

Jenny sighed. Kit might be happy to consult openly, but she felt that from now on these Penarreners would be united in their agreement to oppose him. They had already decided that Kit was an outsider, Penarren-born or not.

Garron noticed her standing there.

'I didn't know you were back!' he said.

Despite the welcome on his face, Jenny recognised Garron's unease.

'Pour yourself a cup of tea and join us, Jenny. Come and hear what folk are saying . . . '

'I'm sorry, Dad, I'd rather keep out of any arguments.'

'You can't avoid this one — someone has to fight for the Chough's future!' Her father's face darkened.

'But that's exactly what I'm doing!' Jenny cried. 'Just because we disagree, you think I must be wrong.

'As I've said many times, the Chough is *my* business! And *I* will decide what's best for it!'

The Morning After

'Nana! Look . . . '

Ben tugged earnestly at a corner of his grandmother's apron. He held a large drawing and a rainbow of crayons in his other fist. Jenny rested her hand on his round head.

'What a lovely picture, Ben! Shall I put it on the wall? Then Mummy can see it before she goes to the doctor's.'

Ben frowned and considered.

'Not finished,' he said at last.

Jenny retied her apron and watched Ben's indomitable blue-dungareed figure wander back to a safe corner of the café. Seeing him settled back to his task, she felt blindly under the counter for cups and saucers until her hands admitted defeat. She bent down and peered properly into the cupboard.

'Dad! Where are the clean cups?' she called.

Garron was in the back room and didn't answer at first. Such was the awkward mood at the Chough that morning Jenny was worried he wouldn't.

'Stacked on top,' he said finally. 'If they had mouths, Jenny, they'd bite you!'

Jenny, about to protest, realised he was right. The stacked cups were reflected in the polished counter-top, and the neat, shiny columns of saucers shone beside them.

'Thanks, Dad!' she said.

She pulled a pile forward and set them out. There was one thing about running the Chough; it never allowed anyone to retreat into silent grumpiness for long. Crockery had to be organised, cutlery polished, cakes baked and sandwiches made. Jenny, wiping teaspoons and rattling them into the saucers, felt these were blessings to be counted this morning, especially after the arguments that had erupted the day before.

Suddenly, there was the crash of a tin

hitting the café floor, and a howl from Ben.

'Don't worry. I'll see to it,' Garron said.

'Thanks!' Jenny responded gratefully. They passed each other in the doorway. Her dad's gaze was less direct than usual. He wasn't smiling, either. She'd lain sleepless for part of last night after their row over Kit's plans. They needed to talk, but it wasn't always easy to catch her father in the right frame of mind.

'Oh, no . . . '

Abandoning a sandwich in mid-spread, she leaned across and flicked the coffee-machine switch off and on. She sighed and tried it again. Touching the side of the machine briefly with one hand, her suspicions were confirmed. It was cold.

'What's wrong now?' she muttered, hearing the irritation in her own voice.

'Want me to look?' Garron volunteered, approaching the counter.

'It was working OK yesterday,' Jenny

told him. 'Surely it wouldn't go wrong for no reason? Just what we need . . . more expense . . . '

She felt Garron's hand warm on her arm.

'It helps if you remember to switch it on at the mains first,' he said. Jenny caught his mock-despairing glance, and smiled.

'Sorry, Dad. Been using you like an emergency crew this morning, haven't I?'

Garron nodded.

'It feels like it!'

He rubbed one hand uneasily back and forth through his hair.

'Jenny, we need to talk.'

'You know what it's like, Dad . . . there's never any time.'

'We must make time. Let me keep an eye on Ben while you heat that batch of pies.'

Garron leaned against the counter and Jenny resigned herself.

'All right, Dad. I'm listening!'

'As I see it, we've got a straight

choice. Allow Kit Venning to do as he pleases in Penarren or stand up for ourselves. In my book, that means standing up for the Chough sooner rather than later!'

Jenny shook her head.

'I don't believe it's as simple as that, Dad. Kit's no tyrant. He's not planning to bulldoze us all into submission.'

'But will he listen to reason?'

'About the children's area, you mean?'

'A playground with kiddies running all over it could cause havoc beside the stream. Anyone can see that! Not to mention installing swings and stuff.'

Jenny turned, a pastry-brush in hand.

'That depends. A children's area might not be a playground, Dad.'

Garron shrugged.

'What else could it be?'

'For instance, is it going to be metal-framed playground equipment, roundabouts and swings and stuff? Or could it be more of a quiet family area, with maybe a hide for bird-watching?

We have to be sure of what we're talking about before we can make any decisions.'

'And who's going to define things? Venning's, of course. They might tell us only what they want us to know.'

Jenny put down the bowl of egg white and sighed inwardly. It was useless with her dad in this mood.

'Well, I think that's a very good argument to stay involved. Then we can make sure Venning's remain accountable to the village. If we opt out, they might think we don't care.'

'Well, I do care. Very much,' Garron growled.

Jenny saw his hands curl into two strong fists on her counter. She recalled the countless times he'd turned out in all weathers to man the lifeboat. And the times he'd returned from a shout, weary and battered.

It never mattered to the former coxswain of the *Etta Trelawney* whether those people who needed him had been foolhardy or brave. He felt duty bound to help anyone in trouble. Of all Penarr-eners, Garron Trelawney had earned the right to say whatever he honestly thought.

'Oh, Dad!' Jenny said, wrapping her floury arms around his neck. 'I know nobody could care more than you! It's just that we see things differently. Let's agree to leave it that way for now, shall we?'

Down To Business

The following morning, Jenny drove up the hill to Trenfos for the promised meeting with Kit. As she left her van and crunched across the gravel drive she straightened her new, business-like jacket. She paused and fastened the buttons; it felt better that way, more formal.

Kit answered the bell.

'Jenny! Thank you for coming. We're in the study. Come and meet Trisha, my assistant . . . '

He ushered her into a wide, pleasant room. A low coffee table occupied the space between three chairs and the rounded settee that hugged the bay window. There was an imposing desk to the other side of the door.

Trisha, at the desk surrounded by papers, looked up and smiled.

'Pleased to meet you, Mrs Hawke,'

she said, shaking Jenny's hand. 'This is a lovely part of the world you live in.'

Jenny gazed through the window down the steep hill to the cove on the left and the harbour to the right, a scene she knew so well.

'Have you had any chance to get to know Penarren?' Jenny asked.

'Not this time. Maybe if I'm needed here again,' Trisha said with a glance at Kit.

Kit smiled but said nothing. Keen to get the meeting underway, he drew a chair forward, and snapped open a file.

'Now,' he said, 'there seems to be fairly strong support for two-thirds of our scheme. The planning applications are already going ahead on those. It's a pity there's opposition to the playground idea from some quarters, but I think that can be overcome. What do you think, Jenny?'

Jenny twisted Dan's silver bracelet on her wrist. It occurred to her that wearing a business-like jacket did not automatically guarantee inner confidence.

'I think,' she said carefully, 'that we should be clear what we're talking about.'

'*An area for children.*' Trisha read the title from a printed sheet.

'I hope you don't mind me saying . . . ' Jenny began. She was surprised when Kit interrupted.

'Let's get this clear,' he said, tapping one finger on the edge of the table. 'No-one needs to apologise for their opinions. I want to be straight with people and tell them honestly what I feel — and I need people to do the same with me. I find that serves me pretty well, as a rule, from business planning to . . . well, getting along with my teenage daughter, I suppose!'

Jenny recalled their recent cliff-top conversation. Suddenly, it felt as if an elastic band had been rolled off a tight package and pinged itself across the floor.

'OK!' Jenny undid one jacket button.

'For a start, you could stop calling it a playground.'

Trisha looked puzzled.

'But surely that's what it'll be? It's the equipment placed inside it that will really matter.'

Jenny shook her head.

'True, but names are important, too. Whenever the word 'playground' is mentioned, people like Morwenna will think of witches' hats . . . '

'Witches' hats?' Trisha enquired.

'A sort of tall cone-shaped round-about. Very heavy. Popular in playgrounds once upon a time. Along with swinging chains on maypoles, and heavy wooden seats.'

'I'm sure we weren't thinking of that sort of equipment,' Trisha said.

'In that case, try to avoid creating the impression that you are,' Jenny advised. 'Go for a more descriptive title. Water Park, Nature Trail . . . something like that.'

'The trouble is, that doesn't sound at all exciting,' Trisha said doubtfully.

'But names are important, I see that,' Kit said. 'We also need to discuss the equipment and materials. We'll have to submit the detailed plans soon, so it might be as well to make some decisions now.'

The discussion became quite technical. Much of it seemed to concern how to install and preserve wooden equipment in a riverside area without using chemicals that would harm plants and animals. Jenny listened, fascinated.

'It's very interesting, but I can see this is all going to take time,' she said at last.

'Anything worthwhile takes time,' Kit said firmly. 'We need to know exactly what kind of equipment we want and how to get it to the site in the first place without causing havoc.'

'My son knows a lot about transport and the local environment. And my dad!' Jenny said eagerly. 'I could ask them.'

'I'll ask them myself,' Kit said, sounding edgy. 'I find a direct approach works better.'

'Well, I don't!' Jenny said.

Kit frowned, but Jenny held his gaze.

'You don't know my dad like I do,' she said at last.

Kit burst out laughing.

'All right, Jenny. Having asked for your honest opinion, it would be foolish of me not to listen to it!'

'Thank you,' Jenny said, feeling more relieved than she dared show. She was beginning to find it easier to speak out.

Trisha glanced at her watch.

'Kit, I shall have to leave soon,' she said.

Kit clapped a hand to his head.

'I forgot! That's what being at home again has done for me. I don't keep to my usual timetable. I'm sorry, I mustn't hold you up . . . '

He signed some letters quickly and folded papers into a file. Trisha tidied them into a briefcase, said her good-byes, and went to retrieve her coat.

Assuming the meeting was over, Jenny made to leave, too.

'Will you stay for coffee?' Kit asked.

'Thanks, that would be very welcome.' Jenny accepted with a smile.

Exciting News!

Kit saw Trisha to her car, and returned to the study with a tray a few minutes later.

'These aren't quite up to Chough standards!' he confessed, proffering a plate of biscuits.

'I have a secret ally. Lily sometimes bakes for me.' Jenny smiled. 'Now, was there something else you wanted to talk about?'

'It's Beatrice,' Kit said, coming to the point. 'She'll be here at the end of the week. I wanted to ask you a favour . . . '

'Ask away.' Jenny grinned.

'I'll understand if you tell me you have to refuse, but I'd like to think Bea could come to you if there was anything worrying her.'

'I'm sure she'd want to speak to you first,' Jenny said.

Kit nodded.

'I hope so. But I thought if I could introduce her to you as a friend, she'd feel better about being here. Especially in view of my other piece of news.'

'What news?' Jenny asked, although she realised what it must be as soon as she'd spoken.

'I've been accepted for training on the *Etta*!' Kit said proudly. 'I've even got a lifeboat pager already!' His face lit up with boyish excitement.

'Congratulations, Kit. Lily mentioned you'd volunteered.'

'Of course, it's more a matter of turning up regularly and showing reliability at first, before I'd ever get chosen for a shout. But I'd hate Bea to feel abandoned if I had to leave her to rush off down the end of the harbour. So do you think you could befriend her?'

'There'll always be someone at the Chough,' Jenny assured him.

'I'm really looking forward to answering that first shout!' Kit said.

Jenny wondered if he'd feel the same if he ever had to return home alone after a loss at sea.

'My father was coxswain of the *Etta* for years,' she reminded him with a smile. 'So I reckon you've asked the right family to back you up!'

'I hadn't forgotten!' Kit relaxed as he stirred his coffee.

'One thing my dad says is to avoid weaving too much romance around being a lifeboatman,' Jenny went on thoughtfully.

'Romantic? Me?' Kit laughed. 'You must be thinking of someone else, Jenny. I'm more your determined, realistic sort.'

'Except where Beatrice is concerned, I suspect!' Jenny said. 'But I'm sure it'll be worth all the ups and downs to have her back with you.'

Kit nodded.

'I'm relying on the magic of Penarren to help sort us out,' he said.

He put down his cup.

'Magic, plus someone kind and

sensible like you, of course,' he said seriously.

* * *

Gary hit *Send* on the keyboard and pushed his chair away from the computer. He stood, stretching his arms above his head.

'I've made coffee. Would you like some?' Sophie, Will Gulliver's wife, popped her head round the door of the museum office.

'Yes please, Soph,' he said. 'I love it here, but I can't say this is my favourite part of the work!'

'We're lucky to have you,' Sophie called from her kitchen.

'Is the baby asleep?' Gary asked as Sophie returned with the drinks.

'Alanna's spark out for once,' Sophie said, sipping her coffee. 'I suppose you and Kerensa will be busy with your new little one soon.'

'It's a while yet. Ben keeps us busy.'

'He's a whirlybird, that boy!' Sophie

said with a grin. 'You're lucky to have your mum and grandfather on hand to help out. I miss that, being so far from home.'

'You have lots of friends here.'

'I know, and Will does everything he can, but he's so busy. It's not only this . . . ' Sophie's glance encompassed not only the museum, but also the Gullivers' little shop and the tourist information displays. 'But now there's this Folk Festival coming up as well.'

She dunked a digestive and took a bite.

'You and Will have been planning it for so long — selfishly, I almost hoped it would never happen,' she said.

'I hope it will,' Gary demurred. 'Or that'll be lots of hard work for nothing!'

Homesick

Sophie sighed.

'It's just that I see so little of Will these days. Sometimes I wonder if he's doing too much.'

Gary didn't want to betray his friend's confidence, but Sophie was clearly worried about him.

'It's important to him, Soph, but he hopes it might help you as well.'

'Me?' Sophie's grey eyes were round with astonishment.

'I think Will hopes the more you learn about Penarren life, the more you'll grow to love it here.'

She shook her head slowly.

'Sometimes I feel the coast is so beautiful, I ought to love it. But other times, I just feel empty and so far from home,' she said quietly.

'But now you and Will have a family, not to mention the business, won't you feel more settled?' Gary asked. He gathered some papers, and dropped them in a box marked *Orders Sent*.

'Maybe,' Sophie said. 'But I can't see how sandcastle competitions in the cove or dancing in the streets is going to give me that. It's not fun-days I need, Gary, it's roots.'

An outer door banged, and Will's comfortable frame filled the office doorway. He was carrying a spare chair in from the shop.

'Who's growing roots?' he demanded.

'Sophie may be contemplating it,' Gary said with a smile at Will's wife.

An insistent cry sounded from the rooms over the shop.

'There goes Alanna!' Sophie passed her cup to her husband as she made for the door.

'I'll see to her — ' Will offered, but Sophie was already halfway up the stairs.

Will sighed, and unfolded his chair beside Gary.

'I worry about her, you know. She's so wound up.'

'She says she's homesick, Will.'

'I know,' Will said miserably. 'I wish I could do something.'

'Give it time,' Gary said.

'We'll have to hope the festival makes Sophie feel more at home, won't we?'

'It'll be fine!' Gary said, trying to sound positive. He hoped the strain of organising the festival project wouldn't make things worse between his friends.

'I've got festival posters ready,' Will said briskly, brandishing a disk. 'Do you want to take a look on screen?'

A Stranger in Town

Despite Sophie's homesickness, Gary felt the Gullivers were exactly the sort of newcomers Penarren needed. It was hard these days to imagine the tiny museum beside the harbour without them. But now he was beginning to wonder if Will really was OK himself.

It wasn't till Sophie had mentioned her worries for him that Gary realised his friend didn't talk often about himself. Whenever Will spoke these days, it was always in relation to the business, his hopes for the festival . . . and his concern for his wife.

Will might be a relative newcomer to the village, but he and Gary had become firm friends. He couldn't imagine Will wanting to leave Penarren now — unless, of course, his wife's yearning for her old home forced him to . . .

Saturday morning at the Chough found Jenny searching for her lost silver bracelet with a sinking heart. She knew she'd had it a few days ago, but now, it seemed to have disappeared.

'It's no good,' she muttered to herself, replacing a cushion on the settee. 'I'll have to look later.'

She went to join her father serving customers in the café.

'Look out there!' Garron exclaimed, brandishing a pickle spoon at the widest window. 'She'll never fit that car into that space! I reckon that's how crowded the traffic's going to be if the developers get their way!'

Jenny saw a low, red car edging backwards and trying to squeeze into the one available space. Finally, it came to a stop, more or less in place, with its wheels sticking out.

The girl who emerged wore faded jeans and a crumpled white shirt. The sea breeze swept her long blonde hair across her face. She trapped a few strands behind one ear. Looking quickly around, she made for the main entrance of the Chough.

'Can I help?' Jenny asked as the girl hesitated in the doorway. 'Tea?'

The girl shook her head.

'I'm looking for my dad. Is he here?'

'That depends on who he is . . . ' Jenny smiled.

The girl hitched her bag-strap on her shoulder. Something about the way this tall young woman moved so restlessly made a connection in Jenny's mind.

'You're Kit's daughter, aren't you?' she said, and suddenly found herself the object of intense scrutiny from a pair of clear green eyes.

'How do you know?' the girl asked.

'Your dad told us you were coming. Beatrice, isn't it?' Jenny said, leaving the counter to welcome her.

'Bea,' the girl confirmed. 'So where is my dad?'

'Not here, I'm afraid.'

Bea looked downcast.

'But they told me he was!'

'Who did?'

'The housekeeper at Trenfos,' Bea said.

Jenny detected a wobble in her voice. Bea looked tired, she thought.

'Let me get you a nice cup of tea!' Jenny offered.

'OK. Thanks.' Bea sighed and shut the door. She slid the bag off her shoulder. 'I've been driving since goodness knows what time this morning, and I got to the house and no-one was there. It was just awful. Then I was sent down here, and still he's not around . . .'

This time Jenny clearly heard the anxiety in her voice. She led Bea to a table and promised tea and a pasty to follow.

'The thing is, if he's not at home, and he's not here, then where is he?' Bea asked, catching Jenny's hand.

'One thing at a time,' Jenny said, patting Bea's slender fingers. 'I'm sure he's not gone far. The best thing to do is to stay put and try his mobile. You can use our phone, if you like.'

Happy Reunion

Bea had drunk her tea and was about to ring Trenfos once more, when Kit pushed open the door of the Chough and strode in.

Jenny was serving customers at the far end of the counter.

'There's someone here who thinks she's lost you!' Jenny called, waving, but Kit didn't hear.

As Jenny bustled towards him, Kit reached across the counter and took her hand, placing on to her palm a familiar silver shape.

'My bracelet — thank you!' Jenny gasped, smiling with relief. She noticed Bea get up from her seat.

'Kit,' Jenny warned, 'you're about to receive a hug.'

Kit looked surprised.

'Not from me . . . ' Jenny laughed. 'Look out!'

Bea launched herself at her father, wrapping her arms around his neck.

'I waited ages. You were late!' Kit cried, his voice muffled.

'I wasn't!' Bea protested. 'I got held up on the motorway. Anyway, aren't you glad I'm here?'

Kit's shoulders relaxed.

'Of course I am, darling. Let me look at you. I've missed you so much!'

'This lady looked after me, Dad.'

Kit glanced in Jenny's direction.

'Thank you,' he said with a nod. Then he turned to his daughter. 'Bea, this is Jenny Hawke, who was married to a good friend of mine — you remember me talking about Dan? She makes the best pasties in Penarren, or anywhere else for that matter!'

'I'm already eating one,' Bea said with a grin. 'Come and join me, Dad!'

'She's a striking young woman, Kit. You must be very proud of her,' Jenny said as Beatrice returned to her table.

'I am,' Kit said fondly.

'Now, about that bracelet of yours

. . . is it all right? I found it after you'd left. I knew it couldn't be Trisha's.'

'I can't tell you how grateful I am you found it.'

'Is it special?' Kit asked.

Jenny nodded.

'Dan gave it to me. I must be sure to get the catch repaired.'

'Glad I spotted it, then . . . ' Kit said.

Jenny noticed his gaze stray longingly towards the counter display.

'Lunch?' she asked, waving a pair of tongs in the direction of the pasties.

'I thought you'd never ask!' Kit beamed.

The Shout

He joined Bea at her table. When Jenny returned a moment later with his lunch she saw a concentrated expression fall across his face. He twisted sideways to look at his pager, and Jenny heard the familiar clap of the maroons in the grey skies over the harbour.

'Sorry, Bea. Got to go, sweetheart!' Kit gasped, leaping up. 'Ask Jenny . . . she'll explain . . . '

Bea rushed out after him.

'Dad!' Jenny heard her call. 'What's the matter?'

Jenny followed and caught the girl's arm.

'It's a shout,' she said.

Bea continued to stare across the harbour uncomprehendingly.

'A call-out for the lifeboat, Bea. Your dad's been in training for a while.'

They saw the *Etta* released to rush

down the slipway. The white spray blossomed as the lifeboat hit the water. Jenny wondered if Kit had had his wish to be included on a shout for the first time.

'You mean my dad's on that little boat?' Bea asked.

'It's not so little, close to . . . ' Jenny said.

'But just look at the waves — and all those black clouds!' Bea wailed.

Jenny put a comforting arm around her.

'There's no better ship or crew than the old *Etta*. My dad's been out on her lots of times, Bea. He'll tell you all about it.'

Bea stared at Jenny for a second, then pressed one hand to her mouth, her eyes bright with anxiety.

Jenny felt a surge of annoyance with Kit. Why on earth hadn't he explained to Beatrice he'd joined the lifeboat crew?

One thing was certain; Bea shouldn't stay out in this rising wind a moment longer. Jenny guided Kit's daughter back to the café.

New Recruit

Jenny leaned against the door of the Chough, struggling to shut it against a gust of wind. The glass panes rattled, and Jenny noticed that Beatrice looked pale.

'You're welcome to stay here just now,' Jenny said. 'The crew will probably call in here on their way home, in any case.'

'But how long will they be?'

'There's no way of knowing, Bea. It depends who or what is in trouble.'

Beatrice shuddered.

'It sounds dreadful out there . . . '

'I've heard it worse, believe me!' Jenny said matter-of-factly, securing the door.

The best remedy, Jenny knew, was to keep busy.

'I'd be very grateful if you'd clear the tables . . . as long as you don't mind, that is,' she said.

Bea nodded abstractedly.

The Chough's main windows looked out on to a wild panorama of distant whipped spray and flying black clouds. Bea couldn't tear her anxious eyes away from the view.

'I'll get you an apron and a tray and your dad will be back before you know it,' Jenny said briskly.

She had no doubt the crew on the *Etta* would be safe, but she sympathised with Bea's fears. Kit's daughter had grown up far from the sea and its ways.

Bea relaxed a little, giggling as Jenny helped her to tie an apron.

'How do I look?' Bea asked, twisting for a better look at the large white bow at her back.

'Wonderful!' Jenny said, smiling to see the girl in better spirits.

'What time does your café close?' Bea asked.

'Not yet, but there's always plenty to do, if you don't mind getting stuck in,' Jenny said.

'It'll be fun!' Bea put on a folded white cap, which instantly slipped sideways.

The cutlery and plates were stacked, the coffee machine cleaned and the teacloths bundled for laundering before Jenny spotted Paul's car negotiating its way through the dwindling downpour.

Three figures jumped out and hurried towards the Chough. Kit was beaming, with Paul gently thumping his arm in approval. Jenny didn't have to ask if everything had gone well.

'All OK!' Paul confirmed.

'Thank goodness!' Kit said, following him into the café. 'And I got my chance with the crew!'

Jenny recognised their mood. Even her self-possessed father had been elated like this when he returned from a successful shout.

A tray clattered and Jenny felt a light figure brush past.

Kit opened his arms, and Bea walked into her father's embrace.

'I was so worried about you, Dad!' she said.

'No need,' Paul said. 'He did just fine.'

'I'm cross you never told me ... ' Bea muttered, her face buried in Kit's shoulder.

Jenny knew this wasn't the time or place for such a discussion. She knew Kit and the others would soon suffer the tiring effects of the shout even if they didn't yet show it.

'Bea, dear. Would you mind? We could surely do with some tea ... ' Jenny said quietly.

Bea nodded and stepped back into her new-found rôle as waitress.

'Our Kitto did well,' Paul said generously. 'First time out, you can get real flustered. Everything seems to happen twice as fast as it should!

'At the last minute, the skipper on the stricken boat got his engine going,' he said, still grinning. 'So we were only escorting. But those waves were rough, really rough, I can tell you!'

'We certainly have the best in water sports in the Wild West ... ' Sally said wryly. 'I'm glad we've met your daughter at last, Kit, but we won't linger, if you don't mind. Paul . . . are you coming?'

Jenny saw Paul hesitate and glance at Kit.

'I'd better do what Sal tells me,' he murmured to Jenny with a smile. 'You'll look out for Kit, won't you, Jenny?'

'Of course!' she promised.

'Nobody better for taking care of new recruits than Coxswain Trelawney's daughter!' he said with a wink.

Jenny stowed the last of the tea trays and finished wiping the empty tables before she took a hot tea for herself and went to sit with Bea and Kit.

Dishonest

Kit glanced around the café. 'Everyone's gone except us. I hope we're not outstaying our welcome,' he said.

Jenny shook her head.

'Of course not,' she reassured him.

'You've still not answered my question, Dad!' Bea resumed. 'Why didn't you say you'd joined the crew? It was worrying enough that you weren't at Trenfos, let alone watching you disappear into thin air one moment after I found you!'

Kit ran a hand down his face. Jenny, reading the signs, recognised that his elated mood was probably wearing off.

'I can only say what I told you before, Bea.'

'You always say we must be honest with each other. Well, I don't call it honest when you keep things like that to yourself!'

'I didn't do it deliberately.' Kit stretched his hand across the table.

'I wanted to tell you face to face when you arrived, Bea. But there just wasn't time!'

'Convenient this shout thing happened when it did, then, isn't it?' Bea said.

Jenny was shocked.

'No-one can help when a storm blows, Bea,' she said gently.

Kit's daughter slid the waitress's cap off her head and placed it wordlessly on the table. Kit looked more uncomfortable, and wearier by the minute. Jenny finished her tea and stood up.

'I hope you won't mind if I give you some advice, Kit,' she said. 'Bea's had a long journey, and the afternoon's been pretty eventful for you, too. Just go home and be glad of each other's company this evening. Leave the discussions until tomorrow. Meanwhile, if you'll excuse me, I'll get on before the rest of the family come home.'

Kit pushed back his chair.

'Yes, of course. Jenny. I'm sorry if we've held you up. Thanks for the tea . . . ' he said. 'Come on, Bea. Let's see if our Mrs Pethick up at Trenfos remembers who we are after all this time!'

Eyes downcast, Bea followed her father.

Once outside, Kit waved cheerfully to Jenny. Bea didn't look back. Watching them go, Jenny hoped she hadn't upset the girl even further.

A Change of Plan

The following morning Kit Venning, a breakfast coffee in his hand, wandered into his hallway at Trenfos house. Sunshine flooded the upper landing.

'Are you up yet, Beatrice?' he called. 'I thought you might like a tour of the sights of Penarren after breakfast.'

His daughter appeared at the top of the stairs in jeans and a pink rugby-style shirt. She stopped, hands on hips, looking not a great deal happier than when they'd left the Chough the day before.

'What's wrong, sweetheart?' Kit asked.

'My room, Dad. That's what's wrong!'

'But I thought we agreed it was the prettiest!'

'It is,' Bea said, flicking a strand of blonde hair behind one shoulder. 'But I've decided I'd prefer one at the front, after all. I'd like a view of the cove. If that's OK?'

Kit's heart sank, remembering the trouble they'd had unloading his daughter's belongings the previous night. He sipped his coffee.

'Well?' Bea asked.

It would set them at odds for the entire day to argue now, Kit thought. There was no reason why Bea shouldn't sleep there.

'Fine!' he said at last.

Bea swooped downstairs with her arms outstretched. Kit slid his coffee cup to safety on the polished hall table.

'I knew you'd agree!' she said, hugging her father round the neck. 'You always do . . . '

'I do not!' Kit protested, smiling inwardly because he knew she was right. He gazed fondly at his daughter. Her moods changed like a sea-shimmer, but it was always wonderful when she was happy.

'Do you want help?' he asked.

'Yes, please,' Bea said, running back up the stairs two at a time. 'You can carry my heavy stuff!'

Kit finished his coffee and, easing his shoulders for the task ahead, followed his daughter.

'Have you thought any more about next year, Bea?' Kit asked on his way from Bea's 'old' room with yet another box.

'I don't know!' Bea said shortly. She rattled open a battery of drawers, one after the other.

'Where are the sheets to fit this bed, Dad?' she asked.

'In the ottoman.'

Kit sank on to the mattress.

'We need to discuss your future, Bea.'

'Not now . . . ' Bea shook a sheet vigorously out of its folds and let it billow towards her father. 'Catch the end, Dad, and tuck it in for me, would you?'

Kit pushed the end of one sheet into place thoughtfully. Bea clearly didn't want to talk about this.

Bea shook out a quilt cover.

'Don't you want to hear about Mum's wedding plans?' she asked, changing the subject.

'I hope they're going well,' Kit said diplomatically.

'Oh, you know Mum!' Bea said, winning her battle with the quilt. 'Nothing would dare go wrong, would it? Except — she really wants to come down here and see you first.'

'A month before the wedding? I shouldn't think she'd have time, Bea!'

'What's wrong? Don't you want to see her?'

There was an edge to his daughter's voice. Kit wondered what was coming next.

'Sweetheart, all I'm saying is I'm sure she's very busy right now. I'd never refuse if she wanted to discuss anything important. Especially about you!'

'I can decide my own future, thanks very much!' Bea snapped.

Kit realised their conversation had come full circle, as it often did. If he didn't take care, they'd be arguing again.

'I know that,' Kit said. 'But I hope

that's no reason to avoid discussing it with your old dad first.'

Bea sighed heavily, and shook another pillow into its case.

Trouble Brewing?

Finally, with her bed made, her clothes in the wardrobe and a cane table groaning under the weight of a lamp, a clock-radio and a one-eyed, flop-eared teddy bear, Bea sighed peacefully and gazed around the room.

Kit couldn't suppress a smile.

'I see Mr Tedworthy has stuck by you,' he said.

'Sometimes I feel he's the only one who has!' Bea replied flippantly. Her hand flew to her mouth. 'Oh, Dad! I'm so sorry! Sometimes my tongue runs away with me. I didn't mean . . . '

Kit gave her a hug.

'There's nothing to be sorry for,' he said gently. 'I wouldn't blame you for feeling upset at times. But you know what your mum and I told you when we separated. Although we couldn't go on, neither of us would ever stop loving you . . . '

He felt his daughter nod her head. Her soft blonde hair fell against his shoulder. It seemed no time at all since she had been wearing pigtails.

The telephone shrilled and Kit moved reluctantly to answer it.

'I just knew your work would raise its ugly head before long!' Bea said with a sigh. 'It always does.'

Kit lifted the receiver.

'Hello, hello! Is that Trenfos House?' a familiar, insistent voice asked. 'Beatrice?'

'Melissa! How are you?' Kit replied.

'Very well, thank you. May I speak to our daughter?'

'Sure. She's right here.'

Kit handed Bea the receiver.

'I'll be in the kitchen with another coffee, if you want me,' he whispered in passing, and went downstairs.

What on earth was Melissa up to now?

Going Underground

Jenny slipped the heavy key into the pocket of her apron and pushed at the Chough's cellar door. It creaked open. The stone steps twisted down into the darkness. Everything smelled of dust, damp wood and ancient sacking. Jenny took the large flashlight from a hook beside the door.

'Dad — I'm just going down to the cellar!' she called.

'Will you be long?' Garron answered from behind the café counter. 'Remember I've got a lifeboat fundraising meeting to go to this morning. I have to leave in about an hour . . . '

Jenny paused on the bottom step to see her dad outlined in the doorway.

'I'm taking a closer look at that ventilator in the stonework butting on to the old terrace.'

'It was OK the last time I saw it!'

135

'And when was that?'

'Longer ago than either of us think, I expect!' Garron said, scratching his cheek. 'Shall I come with you?'

Jenny sighed.

'Dad, I need someone behind the counter, if you don't mind!'

Reluctantly, Garron retreated to the café.

A cellar cobweb brushed Jenny's face. She stopped and lifted her torch higher. The rough stones cast odd shadows. Further along, daylight filtered through a deep-set grille. Stepping carefully, Jenny walked over and peered between the slats on to the remains of the terrace. Thankfully, with a few repairs where the metal joined the stonework, this inside area seemed sound.

'Are you sure you don't need me? Kit's daughter's just arrived. I'm sure she'll stand in for a few moments, if I ask her ... ' Garron's voice floated down from the cellar door.

Jenny, exasperated, made a quick mental note of the fittings she would

136

need to make the repairs and went back to join her father in the café.

Garron was right — Bea would, she was sure, be only too happy to hold the fort at the counter, but she would be reluctant to ask her.

★ ★ ★

Only a few weeks into her stay at Penarren, Bea was already on friendly terms with most of the village. On her frequent visits to the Chough Jenny had often seen her chatting with Kerensa and Lily Pinch. She seemed magnetically attracted to the café.

'I really enjoyed helping here that time the lifeboat got called out!' she'd told Jenny wistfully several times. 'You'd only have to ask if you needed an extra pair of hands, and I'd be here like a shot.'

So far, much as she needed extra help, Jenny had avoided making any request. Kit had made it clear that Bea's visit was strictly a holiday — she would soon be settling down to college studies in London.

Noticing Bea's unhappy frown whenever the subject of studies was mentioned, Jenny suspected there might be tension between father and daughter on that subject. She didn't want to add to it by encouraging Kit's daughter to take on a job against his wishes.

Bea, having delivered a few orders for Garron, was currently sitting at a table deep in conversation with Sally Rosewarne's brother.

Daveth Rosewarne owned and ran a successful campsite close to Penarren. Jenny couldn't help noticing how delighted the young man looked to have Bea's company.

Garron Trelawney cleared his throat.

'She's a lovely girl, but I can't say I envy Kit Venning when she's so . . . ' Jenny's father gazed after Bea, searching for the word.

'Wilful?' Jenny suggested. 'Was I ever as much trouble to you, Dad?'

Garron turned to his daughter with a

softer expression.

'You were pretty good at trying to wrap me round your little finger, my maid!'

'But you taught me that coxswains were in charge!' Jenny smiled.

'Maybe that's Kit's problem,' Garron said thoughtfully. 'He's certainly in charge of his business. But I don't see him being as firm with his daughter. His own father wasn't so easy-going, I can tell you!'

'Perhaps that's why Kit wants to be different,' Jenny said. 'By the way, Dad, we're going to need some new fixings for that ventilator in the cellar. I'll get them in Newquay tomorrow morning.'

Hurrying to wash her hands and get back to work, she heard a gale of laughter from Bea, followed by a guffaw from Daveth.

Jenny hoped Kit would approve of his daughter's growing friendship with Sally's brother.

The Penarren Effect

Kit Venning arrived at the Chough twenty minutes later.

'Jenny . . . I'm glad I've caught you. Could you arrange to meet me for a visit to those old harbourside properties tomorrow afternoon? I'd like to hear your ideas before we get started on the work.'

'But that project won't affect the Chough directly,' Jenny protested.

'That's not why I'm asking you — I value your opinion.'

'Let me see . . . Lily will be here all day, but I'll have to ask Kerensa for extra help.' Jenny was still uncertain.

'It would only be for half an hour, and I'd really appreciate it.' Kit paused, eyebrows raised.

Jenny nodded.

'OK. What time?'

'Three o'clock. I have . . . another

meeting at four.' Kit pulled a note from his pocket and glanced at it.

'Fine,' Jenny said.

'I'm also looking for Daveth Rosewarne. He's not here, by any chance?' Kit pushed the note back into his diary and glanced around the café.

Jenny nodded in the direction of the corner table where Daveth and Bea lingered over cups of coffee.

'Is that my daughter?' Kit asked in surprise.

'I thought you were meeting me at the lifeboat station in five minutes, Bea,' he called to her. 'What are you doing here?'

Bea came towards him, smiling.

'I'm on my way, Dad! Guess what — I've been helping Jenny again!'

'Helping?'

'Well, yes, sort of, I helped Coxswain Trelawney with some of the orders . . .' Bea's eyes were sparkling.

'I thought we decided . . .'

'You decided!'

Kit rolled his eyes.

'Look, sweetheart, I don't think we

should have this conversation all over again. Are you coming to see the *Etta* with me, or not?'

'What about Daveth? He said you wanted to speak to him about caravans.'

Kit drummed his fingers on the café counter.

'My darling daughter's only been here a couple of weeks, and already I'm feeling the strain!' he muttered. 'I forgot Daveth was one of the reasons I came in here in the first place!

'Ask him if he fancies a stroll round the harbour to the boathouse, Bea, and we can talk on the way . . . '

Bea went to collect Daveth and Kit turned to Jenny with a sigh. She couldn't help smiling.

'It's known as the Penarren Effect,' she told him philosophically. 'You almost never get things done in quite the way you planned!'

Kit pursed his lips.

'Well, Mrs Hawke, let's hope I'm on track again soon. I'm not good at suffering frustrations.'

A Gift

Next morning Jenny was on her way to Newquay by eight-thirty and had completed her shopping by ten. By then, the sun had broken through the cloud.

She drove back feeling she was seeing the rush of green in the hedges beside the road for the first time. Dan's silver bracelet glinted in the sun. Days like this, she felt, were a gift.

Softly, she began to sing a song she'd learned as a child.

'Silver buckles on his knee,' she hummed.

She bounced over the hill at the top of the valley.

'He'll come back and marry me . . . '

Penarren, granite-grey and sea-blue, sparkled in the dip far below.

It was too good an opportunity. She

wouldn't be needed at the Chough for at least another hour. She decided she would drop off the shopping quickly then take a walk beside the river.

Stolen Moments

A short time later, Jenny set off in the direction of the cove. The ground roughened beneath her feet until she found herself on the beach. Beside her, the stream ran to the sea and the rocks stuck up out of the firm, damp sand.

The sea air patted her face. She slid down against a rock and shook out her shoes. Then she tilted her head back against the granite, and held her eyelids half closed so the rainbows could cling to her eyelashes.

'Hi!' Paul Biddick stood squarely on the sand, blocking out the sun and the rainbows.

'Hello, there! I had a few minutes and couldn't resist playing truant,' Jenny said, smiling. She put one hand above her eyes to see him properly.

'I wasn't sure it was you,' he said. 'I was on my way back from the lifeboat

145

and spotted you — surely that can't be Jenny relaxing for once, I thought!'

'I can't think what you mean,' Jenny protested with a laugh. 'I'm sure I've been known to chill out on the beach before . . . '

Paul chuckled.

'Remember when we were kids, Jenny?' he asked. 'Barefoot on this beach all summer long. Least, that's how I remember it!'

Jenny wriggled her toes and nodded.

'I was just thinking about the caves,' she said, waving an arm to her left. 'Wondering how soon it will be before little Ben plays explorers there just like we did!'

Paul seemed reluctant to leave.

'Mind if I join you?' he asked eventually.

Jenny shifted obligingly. For a few minutes, they sat side by side, listening to the waves.

'Been polishing up the *Etta*?' Jenny asked.

'Paperwork,' Paul said briefly. 'Glad

to get it over with!'

'I suppose it's not so bad when it's for something worthwhile.'

'True, but the *Etta*'s not the only woman in my life, you know!' Paul grinned.

'C'mon!' Jenny said, suddenly impish. 'Let's see if the caves look the same as they did when we were kids!'

She jumped up, feeling her heels dig into the damp sand. When she reached the meandering shallows of the stream crossing the beach, she stopped.

'The water's *freezing*!' she squealed.

Paul laughed, pointing gleefully at his sturdy boots.

Jenny waited for him at the mouth of the cave that had seemed so enormous when they were children.

'Good to know it's still here,' Paul said, catching up. 'What with everything else in the village changing . . .'

'I suppose you'll be looking for your own place now you're full-time with the *Etta*,' Jenny said.

Paul shook his head.

'I'd like to, but it's tough, you know that — watch out, Jenny!' he cried as her bare foot slipped on the wet rock.

Jenny grabbed at his arm.

'Whoa!' Paul said with a grin. 'Lifeboat to the rescue!'

His familiar bear hug encircled her, held her safe, and then deepened. Jenny felt a heartbeat. For a moment she couldn't tell whose it was . . .

Surprised, she felt Paul's gentle touch as he guided her face to his.

They'd kissed many times, but never like this. Yet she felt oddly detached. She recalled it must be lunchtime.

'I should go . . . really . . . ' Jenny murmured, one hand still on Paul's shoulder.

'Not yet,' he said, his arms tightening around her.

But all the same, after she'd lightly returned his kiss, she was relieved he didn't stop her. Her feet barely felt the chilly water this time as she retraced her steps across the stream.

Cornish Caution

Kit phoned the Chough early next morning to ask if Jenny could meet him earlier than arranged. After some hasty replanning on Jenny's part, she made her way across the square a couple of hours later to find Kit already standing near the harbour wall, glancing at his watch.

'I hope I'm not late,' Jenny said.

Kit smiled, a quick yet reassuring smile.

'It's good of you to fit this in,' he said. 'Unavoidable change of plan.'

The battered buildings loomed before them.

'Is it safe?' Jenny asked, peering through the doorway.

'We've got the official go-ahead,' Kit told her. 'We start the outside work on Monday,' he said, indicating a stack of wooden props against a far wall, 'but it's quite safe.'

'Why do you need my opinion?'

'I'm looking for ideas for how we should use the space inside,' Kit replied. 'Design, and so on.'

Jenny stepped across the threshold. The dust rose and made her sneeze.

'Aren't you going to tell me what's been decided already?' she asked, searching for a hankie.

She was doing her best to concentrate. Paul's kiss on the beach the previous afternoon had filled her mind with concerns other than plaster and paint.

'I don't want to influence you!' Kit grinned.

He glanced briefly at his watch.

Jenny wasn't in the mood for guessing games.

'I'm sure I can still think for myself, whatever someone else has already said,' she murmured.

'The less I say the better,' Kit insisted.

'Do you always do this?'

'What?' Kit asked mildly.

'Circle round a topic, until you get

the response you want? I feel like a fish on a line!' Jenny protested.

Kit laughed outright.

'I'm told it's what I'm good at,' he admitted. 'But I hope you won't leave in a huff now you've rumbled me!'

He grinned broadly and Jenny felt herself smiling back.

She moved around him, tilting her head to gaze at the flaking paint. Cobwebs stirred gently in the air in one corner, and beneath the broken ceiling opposite she could see exposed laths.

'Will you alter your plans if my ideas are different?' she asked.

'Nothing is set in stone,' Kit assured her.

He raised his brows in anticipation.

'You'll have to wait.' Jenny held up her hand. 'I want a proper look.'

'It's your Cornish caution I'm counting on,' Kit said with a smile.

'I suppose running the Chough on a shoestring for years has at least taught me that,' Jenny agreed ruefully.

Kit strolled ahead. He paused to check his watch again.

Since he offered no opinions, Jenny was determined to take all the time she needed to reach her own. For the next half-hour she peered at window-frames, lintels, ceilings and floors, pausing occasionally to rub a surface or tap a wall.

Finally she halted, gazing at yet another battered door frame.

'Well?' Kit asked.

'The ground is at such different levels,' Jenny observed.

'So you'd keep the three units separate?'

Jenny nodded.

'Knocking them through would spoil the whole set-up, anyway, in my opinion,' she said.

Kit pushed one hand through his fair hair, listening intently.

'You could rent units separately for craft displays, tourist information, artwork . . . Small scale — big impact!' Jenny added, with a rush of enthusiasm.

'I wondered how you'd see it . . . ' he murmured.

'I bet you were hoping to make it one huge modern art gallery!'

'Not this time,' Kit said, grinning. 'I don't want to rebuild completely unless I can help it.'

He hesitated.

'Jenny . . . is something wrong? You seem distracted,' he began. 'Are you worried about leaving them to manage at the Chough this morning?'

Jenny felt herself blushing. She didn't want to tell Kit how much Paul had occupied her thoughts since yesterday.

'My timetable's been upset less than yours, I imagine!' she said, trying to keep her voice light. 'Luckily, both Bea and Lily offered to help at the Chough today . . . '

She watched Kit push his fingers into his hair again, something she was beginning to realise he did when he was uneasy.

'It's all under control,' she added, noticing Kit checking his wrist once more. 'But I'm beginning to wonder whether I should ask you the same question.'

Kit glanced at her quizzically.

'Is there anything wrong with that timepiece, Kit, or is something bothering *you*?'

Peace

Gary had found the atmosphere in Gulliver's shop tricky all morning. Will and Sophie had been up half the night with Alanna, who was teething. He'd offered to hold the fort for a couple of hours to give Will and Sophie a break. Sophie had been keen, but not Will. He said he couldn't afford to ease up so close to the festival and stalked off to the shop.

By lunchtime, Gary felt the Gullivers could do with an hour to themselves. He shut down his computer.

'I'll be within hollering distance if you need me,' he said.

Will barely looked up from his pile of papers.

Outside, Gary felt as if a heavy rucksack had tumbled from his shoulders. He leaned on the harbour rail and looked out to sea, letting the waves calm him before settling himself on a nearby bench.

A short distance away, he saw his mother and Kit Venning leave the row of three semi-derelict buildings and head back across the square. Kit stopped on the way to take a call on his mobile phone.

'Hi!' Jenny greeted her son as she drew near. She slid on to the seat beside him. 'Good Chough pasty?'

'The best!' Gary said with a grin. Wordlessly, he offered her his apple, but Jenny shook her head.

'I'll have my lunch when I get back, thanks all the same, love. How are Will and Sophie?'

Gary pulled a face.

'Arguing a bit. Lack of sleep. I gather the baby's teething.'

Jenny grunted in sympathy and tilted her face to catch the sun. She took a few moments then patted Gary on the shoulder.

'I must go!' She sighed. 'It'd be lovely to stay, but . . .'

Gary peeled a banana and grinned.

'Tell me about it . . .'

A Sense of Perspective

He watched her walk away, and stretched out his legs one at a time. He wished Will and Sophie would take a leaf out of his book. It was good to take a little time out in the fresh air. Gary finished his lunch, leaned back, and closed his eyes. He never understood why people rushed when life improved if you took it at a slower pace.

He heard a shuffle nearby and opened one eye. Kit stood with one hand tenting his gaze.

He couldn't help feeling worried — he hadn't seen Kit to speak to since their confrontation at the village meeting.

'Hello,' Kit said pleasantly.

'I hear you got your first shout on the *Etta* . . . ' Gary said, steering well away from contentious topics such as planning applications.

'I did!' Kit agreed with a smile.

'Must have been quite an experience,' Gary said.

'You've never thought of joining the crew?'

Gary shook his head.

'My dad had enough daring for everyone in our family,' he said. 'I never felt I could compete!'

'It doesn't necessarily mean you have to climb a cliff-face. 'They also serve who only stand and wait' ... ' Kit quoted.

'I didn't think you'd know Milton,' Gary blurted out. Immediately he regretted his outspokenness. 'Sorry, Mr Venning. What I mean is ... '

Kit took a seat beside Jenny's son.

'There's a lot we don't know about each other. But despite what you might think, I'm really not aiming to wipe out Penarren's wildlife!'

'That's a relief!' Gary smiled politely. 'But you were so certain of your plans at that meeting,' he went on tentatively. 'It made the rest of us look as if we hadn't one good idea between us.'

He cleared his throat; he'd introduced the very topic he'd meant to avoid.

'But everyone has their own ideas!' Kit exclaimed. 'And at that meeting you weren't afraid to say so.'

'I felt it would have been worse to keep quiet,' Gary said. 'No-one can have all their own way.'

'Quite right, too!' Kit said.

'You like arguments?' Gary said in surprise.

'I like a good debate.' Kit leaned back to study Gary's face.

'You know, you and your mum are very alike in some ways.'

'Just as well for you we took different sides, then,' Gary said.

'The differences aren't as big as you might imagine,' Kit said warmly. 'For instance: should the riverside development be called a playground?'

Gary frowned.

'Isn't that what you want?'

'It could be a bird hide!' Kit said.

'If that's what you're thinking of, I

might be happier,' Gary agreed.

'Can you guess who insisted on clearer descriptions?'

Gary knew, but waited.

'Your mum!' Kit said triumphantly. 'She's been my strongest influence.'

'Have you got planning permission for that area yet?' Gary asked. He tried not to show his relief when Kit shook his head.

'That's been applied for separately to avoid holding up the other work,' Kit said.

'So there's a chance it won't happen?' Gary asked.

'On the contrary, I'm sure it will,' Kit said. 'But whatever happens, we need your opinions, Gary. I promised I'd listen to everyone and, believe me, I mean it.'

Kit got to his feet, tall, smiling and confident.

The early afternoon sunlight bounced off the choppy little waves in the harbour behind him. Although Gary smiled a farewell, he couldn't shake off a feeling of unease.

This man was so unlike Gary's father — he wondered how they'd been so close. But Kit's dynamism was recognisably similar to Dan Hawke's and that was enough to put Gary on his guard.

There was the Newquay job to consider, too. If he was successful, he and Kerensa would have to move. But he didn't want Kit Venning to assume he'd lose all interest in Penarren if he went . . .

★   ★   ★

Gary returned to Gulliver's and walked into a kitchen smelling of tomato soup. He felt something grip his knees.

'Daddy, Daddy!' Ben shrieked.

Gary swept his giggling son into his arms.

'What are you doing here?' he asked.

'I came with Auntie Sophie!' Ben shouted, squirming delightedly. 'I had a yummy dinner!'

Will's wife was at the table spooning food into Alanna.

'That was very kind of you, Soph,' he said, depositing Ben back on the floor. 'Was there a problem, or did you fancy borrowing a boy-whirlwind for the afternoon?'

'I thought he might as well eat here after playgroup since Kerensa was so busy,' Sophie Gulliver said with her small smile. 'She said you'd take him home later.'

Gary nodded and swiftly fielded a fidgety Ben from under Sophie's chair.

'He can help me tidy the office while you're giving the baby her lunch,' he said, holding on to his son's hand.

'I only hope he behaves himself . . . ' Gary muttered as his son rolled to the floor again.

Gary had heard rumours that most children came home from playgroup in need of a nap. He'd often wished that his son was one of them.

Mother and Child Reunion

Kit Venning was checking the arrivals board at the station, so he heard rather than saw the moment when Bea caught sight of Melissa.

'Mum!'

His daughter shot from his side and ran the length of the platform, arms outstretched and baggy T-shirt flapping.

Melissa, sleek and smart in a pale turquoise trouser suit, lifted her hand to bring Derek and the trolley bearing her luggage to a halt beside her.

'Darling!' Melissa cried, embracing Bea. 'How I've missed you!'

Derek stepped smiling from behind the suitcase trolley and offered a firm handshake to Kit and Beatrice.

'Say hello to Mum, too, won't you, Dad?' Bea said, tucking her arm firmly through Melissa's.

'Hi,' Kit said quietly. He hesitated,

and then he dropped the briefest kiss on Melissa's cheek. She was wearing a perfume he remembered.

'Kitto,' Melissa murmured warmly. 'The least I expected this time was an honour-guard of lifeboatmen!'

'Can't expect that, Melissa, darling,' Derek said. 'Poor chap would be weighed down with no end of ropes and whistles!'

Kit smiled and shook his head.

'It's not quite as bad as Derek thinks, but sorry to disappoint you all the same, Mel.'

'At least you're properly dressed, Kitto. What on earth has Beatrice thrown on today?' Melissa stepped back on one elegant heel to take in the full effect of her daughter's outfit.

The answer was almost lost as Kit and Bea both rushed to explain.

'Bea was helping out at a local café when I collected her . . . '

'It's just an old top. I didn't want to spoil my new one.'

The horrified look on Melissa's face

stopped them both.

'Beatrice? Working in a greasy sea-front café?' she demanded.

'Not exactly . . . ' Kit was determined to avoid an argument in front of Derek before they'd even reached the car.

'The Chough's not greasy!' Bea interrupted earnestly. 'Kerensa's my friend, and she was very busy this morning because Dad and Jenny had a meeting. Jenny's very nice, too. So there's absolutely nothing to worry about. And they make the best pasties at the Chough, Mum. You must try one!'

Melissa's expression softened. She tidied a strand of her daughter's hair.

'Perhaps I will, darling!' she said. 'What do you think, Derek?'

Derek eased the collar of his shirt again and cleared his throat.

'I'm not sure . . . ' he said. 'I might prefer a proper meal somewhere.'

'But a pasty is a proper meal!' Bea protested. 'It used to be savoury at one end and sweet at the other. Daveth said so!'

'Who's Daveth?' Melissa asked as they reached the car park.

'Sally's brother,' Bea replied. 'Sally's on the lifeboat, too, and she's Jenny's friend . . . '

'Goodness, what a lot of friends you've made in such a short time!' Melissa exclaimed. 'We're going to need weeks to meet them all, aren't we, Derek, dear?'

Treat

Kit and Derek stowed the cases and managed to close the boot at the second attempt.

'Is it far to the Four Winds, Kitto?' Melissa asked as Kit selected first gear.

'The Four Winds Hotel? I thought I was taking you to Trenfos?'

Melissa shook her head.

'But there's tons of room at home!' Bea cried.

'We didn't want to put either of you to any trouble,' Melissa said. 'Besides, Derek wanted to spoil me.'

Not for the first time, Kit acknowledged to himself gratefully that Derek understood Melissa very well.

'The Four Winds it is, then!' Kit said.

'It's very posh,' Bea said approvingly. 'You'll have great views, Mum. I hope we can visit you lots.'

'I agreed with Melissa that we should

all have dinner there tonight,' Derek put in. 'My treat!'

★ ★ ★

Once Derek and Melissa had booked in and changed, Kit drove everyone back to Penarren Cove. The scenery unfolded along the coast road like the unwrapping of a special gift.

'Mum and I want to go to the beach,' Bea said urgently. 'And Derek wants to as well, don't you, Derek?'

Derek was sitting behind him, so Kit couldn't see his expression. Bea's impatient muttering continued, however.

Kit squeezed to a halt near Gulliver's shop to let his passengers out, but there was nowhere to park.

'Let's meet back at the Chough car park in a couple of hours,' he told everyone. 'I've got one or two visits to make in Penarren . . .'

'You haven't changed! I guessed you'd be as busy as ever, Kitto,' Melissa said. 'I'm sure Beatrice will look after us — I'm longing to find somewhere to paddle!'

The two women slid elegantly out of Kit's car and headed for the beach. Bea, giggling, linked arms with Melissa and tugged her mum along the small path to the sandy cove. The two women disappeared in a swirl of blue and yellow silk and toning primrose-coloured bags.

At the hotel, Melissa had unpacked one of her most glamorous silky tops and persuaded Bea to wear it.

'Beatrice and her mother could be mistaken for sisters in those outfits,' Derek said, gazing at Melissa in admiration.

He set off after them, slithering awkwardly in the soft sand.

Kit couldn't help a pang of sympathy for Melissa's fiancé. Derek didn't look at all at ease, even in his brand-new casual green polo shirt. He must be longing to be back in the City.

Still, Kit thought, at least they were only down for the weekend — although

Melissa hadn't confided in Kit exactly how long she and Derek hoped to remain in Penarren. Kit had been quietly relieved later when Derek himself told him they planned to be back in London on Monday.

A Step Too Far

The Chough car park was busy again. The only space Kit could find was at the rear of the building. Once out of the car he paused and listened. He could hear the song of the little stream running over the stones beside the old terrace on its way to the sea. He breathed deeply for a few moments, enjoying the peace.

Terrace Meeting

During the next two hours, Kit met builders and suppliers, spoke to Fred Trudgian and his stalwart sons at the Merrymaid about work-rates, and chatted with Lily Pinch as she left for home after her stint at the Chough.

The sun was slipping beneath a thin, dark cloud and glittering on the distant waves as he made his way back to his car. He heard the creaking café sign and glanced up to see the red-legged Chough shining in the late rays of sunlight.

Jenny was standing slightly above him, on the Chough's terrace.

'This catches the evening sun well!' he called.

'Mind the old steps, if you want to come up and have a look!' Jenny called back.

Kit tested the handrail as he climbed,

but stopped when he saw Jenny's worried expression.

'It's strong enough, as long as you don't shake it about. It's next on my list of repairs,' she said.

Kit strolled to the edge of the paving and peered over the edge into the rough grasses beyond. He could still hear the stream.

'So this is where you'll be expanding the café?' he asked.

'Yes,' Jenny said.

'Perhaps to accommodate all those extra visitors on the way to and from the children's area?' he suggested.

'Perhaps,' she agreed.

'You're sounding cautious again!' he teased.

'I can't get things moving as quickly as I'd like,' she told Kit seriously. 'But I need to get started if I want my business to take advantage of the extra tourists.'

Kit paced across the stones, and stood thoughtfully in front of her.

'I'd like to help . . . ' he said at last.

Jenny turned away.

'Thank you. But absolutely not, Kit.'

'Jenny, I'm not being kind. If people knew they could find excellent food nearby after an interesting visit, it would be to everyone's advantage.'

Jenny suddenly looked him full in the face. Her expression warned him not to continue.

'This is my café, Kit. *Mine*. I don't want or need anyone else taking responsibility.'

'I'm hardly proposing a takeover,' Kit said reasonably.

'It's not that. I say exactly the same to my dad when he gets big ideas.'

Kit nodded. It might be best to leave the topic for now. But he doubted it would disappear from his mind entirely.

★ ★ ★

The sun began to melt into the sea as three other figures waved from the car park below. They climbed the protesting wooden steps.

'Hi, Dad!' Bea greeted her father cheerfully, reaching the top. Melissa appeared next, then Derek, who was stoically carrying all the bags. Everyone stopped to take in the terrace scene illuminated by the setting sun.

'Isn't it wonderful up here? What other secrets have you kept from me about Penarren, Kitto?' Melissa asked lightly.

She shaded her eyes and seemed to notice Jenny for the first time. Smiling, she sailed towards her.

'And you must be Mrs Hawke! Beatrice told me all about you this afternoon,' Melissa said, taking Jenny's hand. 'It seems I must try a true Cornish pasty before I leave Penarren or my education is not complete.'

'I'll make sure you have one on the house!' Jenny laughed.

Kit watched in wonder. It wasn't a surprise to him that people generally took to Jenny Hawke, but he knew Melissa wasn't always so easy-going.

'It was such a comfort,' he heard

Melissa saying to Jenny, 'to know Beatrice had someone sensible she could turn to while she was here . . . '

'Apart from Dad, of course!' Bea put in, taking Kit's arm.

'But we all know men don't think of everything,' Melissa said crisply. Then her face softened, and she glanced at Kit from under her eyelashes.

'Not that I'm blaming you in any way, Kitto. But you know how much I worried about our daughter spending the entire summer in a place where she didn't know anyone.'

'I think Bea has put that right for herself,' Jenny said quietly. 'I've never known anyone make so many friends of all ages in such a short time.'

'It's just a gift I have!' Bea laughed happily. 'Wouldn't you say so, Dad?'

'Among many others . . . ' Kit said fondly.

'Which is why we're hoping she'll make the best of them and continue her studies. Aren't we, Kitto?' Melissa looked around the group.

There was a familiar challenging note in her voice that Kit recognised only too well.

'Perhaps this isn't the time for that discussion,' Kit said, keeping his tone light. 'And certainly not if it's going to be on an empty stomach!'

He glanced at Derek. Fortunately Melissa's fiancé understood. He made a show of consulting his watch.

'We'll need to get our skates on if we're having dinner at the hotel this evening, Melissa, darling!' Derek said. 'I hope you'll excuse us, Mrs Hawke.'

What About Me?

'Dinner at the Four Winds! How nice of old Derek to treat us!' Bea said. They'd taken Melissa and Derek back to their hotel, and had returned to Trenfos to change.

Bea paused from styling her hair in the bathroom.

'I'd prefer it if you didn't call him 'old Derek', Bea!' Kit chuckled from the landing. 'For one thing, he's soon going to be your stepfather. And for another, you know he's not much older than I am!'

'He always seems much older than you, Dad!'

'Even so, sweetheart . . . '

'I know.' Bea sighed. She unpinned her hair and reached for a comb. 'But I can't help how I feel.'

'Neither can your mother. She has feelings too, and she loves Derek, don't forget.'

Bea froze, comb in hand.

'It sounds weird when you say it like that, Dad.'

'It's up to your mum if she wants to be with someone again, Bea.'

'Or if she decides she doesn't!' Bea drew the comb through her hair until it crackled. 'After all, Dad, if she fell out of love with you, then she might do the same with Derek after a while . . . and then . . . '

Kit's throat closed. He knew where Bea's thoughts were leading.

'And then, perhaps she'll want to be with us again . . . ' came his daughter's voice, trailing and vulnerable.

Kit shrugged himself into his jacket, and waited on the landing until Bea put down her comb. Then he leaned over and kissed her forehead.

'You know we'd be deceiving ourselves to think that will ever happen, my darling. I'm happy as I am, and your mum and Derek certainly are . . . '

'But what about me?'

Bea had gone downstairs ahead of

him and was looking up from the bottom step. Kit was glad to see she'd decided to leave her hair falling prettily around her shoulders.

'After the past few weeks here in Penarren, I can't believe you're the only one who's not happy!' Kit said.

★   ★   ★

He was relieved to see Bea, in one of her lightning changes of mood, flash him her widest smile.

'For once, you're right, Dad! It's been great meeting Daveth — and all my other friends,' she admitted.

'Then it's time to consider Derek sometimes, my sweetheart. For your mum's sake — and because it's plain good manners.'

Bea grinned.

'I promise I'll even keep my cool this evening when Mum tells me I should have pinned my hair up after all. OK, Dad?'

A Change of Plan

The restaurant at the Four Winds was a marvel of silence and discretion. Even the clink of the elegant cutlery was muffled on the thick tablecloths.

'Where have Mum and Derek got to?' Bea asked, looking around.

'They don't seem to be here yet,' Kit said. 'Not to worry. I don't suppose anyone will mind if we go in. Derek's booked the table.'

The menus arrived inside embossed leather folders. Kit smiled as Bea bent her head and concentrated on the serious business of deciding what to eat.

'What do you fancy?' he asked at length.

Bea considered.

'I haven't decided yet, Dad . . . '

Kit glanced at the doorway into the busy restaurant several times.

'I'll have the fish, I think.' Bea looked up at last from her menu. 'Now . . . where *are* those two . . . ?'

At that moment, Kit saw Melissa heading for their table. He stood up.

'Mel!'

She met his gaze, her face pink and her eyes bright. Kit knew that look, and it worried him.

'We're ready to order . . . Is everything all right?' Kit asked.

'No,' Melissa said shortly.

'What's happened, Mum?'

'Derek . . . ' Melissa sat down abruptly and fumbled a handkerchief from her handbag. With an effort, she regained control of her voice.

'I wanted to stay at least another fortnight. He said it was out of the question, even for my daughter's sake. He didn't actually like Cornwall much, he said.' She dabbed at her eyes.

'Oh, Mum,' Bea said, sliding sympathetic fingers around Melissa's arm. 'But it's so lovely here . . . '

'I told him so, too, but for some

reason he couldn't — or wouldn't — agree.' Melissa bravely squared her shoulders. 'Derek has returned to his City life . . . We've never spoken like that before . . . '

Melissa reached her free hand towards Kit. Her expression was both sweet and sad, and he had to admit he didn't quite know what to make of it.

'Kitto,' she said softly. 'I've decided to postpone my wedding. I'd like to stay in Penarren for a while . . . '

A Grand Day Out

'Out and about with our mobile radio station this morning, ladies and gentlemen, we're glad to welcome Coxswain Trelawney aboard!'

A blonde journalist with a sharp, pretty face stepped forward to interview Garron.

'*Retired* coxswain . . . ' he said politely, and the girl smiled.

'Would you like to tell our listeners what's happening at Penarren's Folk Festival this week?' the girl continued smoothly, holding out the microphone.

'It was all Will Gulliver's idea, really,' Garron said, shifting the peak of his cap. 'He's the one from Gulliver's museum and shop over there . . . '

'But you were among those up really early this morning to start things off, weren't you?'

'Couldn't help myself!' Garron said,

grinning. 'Someone was walloping that big ol' drum at the crack of dawn — I don't think anyone in Penarren was asleep after that!'

'It's certainly loud!' the girl said, covering one ear as the drums crashed.

Garron took a deep breath and raised his voice to be heard over the band instruments tuning up.

'It's going to be a great few days,' he said. 'Today, on the beach, we've got games for the kiddies and a bouncy castle, not forgetting the sandcastle competition this afternoon, then around the harbourside we've got stalls selling good Cornish food all day.'

'And around the village, Mr Trelawney?'

'Well, there's an Art and Craft Exhibition up at the village hall all week — you can even try your hand at a potter's wheel! There will be poetry readings this afternoon in the yard at the Merrymaid. All kinds of music playing throughout the week, and garden plants on sale at Lily Pinch's cottage.'

'And we're all looking forward to the

grand procession at nine o'clock from here by the harbour!' the reporter added, moving aside quickly as a player whirled dangerously close.

Garron ducked in sympathy. Penarren certainly needed to be awake this morning!

'Is your family here, too?' the interviewer asked.

Garron waved towards groups of people gathering on the paths, while others settled on sunny seats and walls.

'My daughter's busy at the Chough café,' he said. 'But my grandson and his family are here somewhere.'

'So it's a great family day out, you'd say?'

'Certainly.'

Rumours

Garron drew a deep breath, determined to get all his information across.

'And the crew will never forgive me if I don't mention the *Etta!* On Saturday, our final day of the festival, we've got a fair with tombola, hoopla and more games on the beach, and visitors will also be able to enjoy a demonstration by the famous Penarren lifeboat,' he finished.

Again, the drums compressed the air around them so Garron didn't quite catch what his interviewer asked next. He did hear the words 'new developments'.

'Those renovated buildings along o' the harbour?'

The interviewer nodded.

'I think they'll prove their worth,' he said thoughtfully into the microphone. 'Been an eyesore for too many years, is my opinion!'

'So — our retired coxswain supports the changing face of Penarren? Does that apply to the river developments on the other side of the village, too?' the blonde girl asked.

The band abruptly circled away from the radio van, leaving Garron's ears ringing.

'Not quite,' he said, clearing his throat in the comparative lull. He felt a warning prickle across the back of his neck. This question wasn't quite so simple to answer.

'But surely providing somewhere for children must be a priority, especially if you're hoping to attract tourists?'

'Not if it causes more problems than it solves.'

'Our information from Vennings is that work begins soon. What's your reaction?'

Garron shook his head. It was still a heated topic in the village, yet this didn't seem like the right time or place to bring the matter up. He had intended only to publicise the festival.

Then he caught sight of Gary's face in the crowd. He must say something on his grandson's behalf.

'It's like this . . . ' Garron said, leaning towards the microphone. 'My grandson and his group have done a lot of work — voluntarily and in their own time, mind — to keep that particular spot just as it should be for the plants and wildlife down there. And we're being watchful, that's all. We don't want that work put in danger.'

'So it's not the case you're simply looking to preserve the idyllic view from your daughter's café? Because there's also a strong rumour she'll be renovating the terrace up there pretty soon, isn't there?'

Garron coiled the rope more tightly and felt it bite into his fingers.

'I'm afraid I can't rightly comment,' he muttered.

'But you'd prefer the playground idea to be abandoned?'

The former coxswain took another deep breath and nailed his colours to the mast.

'Yes,' he agreed finally. 'If you want a straight answer, I would prefer that no-one builds there. I'll keep doing my utmost to see that it don't happen!'

Intervention

There was a rustle. Garron turned to catch sight of Melissa stepping up behind him on to the low platform of the mobile radio van.

'Might I say something . . . ?' she asked from behind Garron's shoulder. She squeezed past as Garron moved back.

'And you are . . . ?' the interviewer asked, switching the microphone from one to the other.

'Melissa Watson. I'm only a visitor to Penarren, but I've been helping a lot with the festival. I don't know everything that's been said, but in my opinion Penarren needs a safe playground for children.'

'So you'd be in favour?'

'I know when my daughter was small, we always loved the swings and roundabouts and things, didn't we, Beatrice?'

Garron glanced at Bea who was standing nearby with Daveth Rosewarne. She had turned pink and looked embarrassed.

'But we don't know exactly what's planned yet, do we, Mum?' she called.

The pretty blonde interviewer looked from mother to daughter, then shifted the microphone decisively.

'Perhaps you'd like to reply, Mr Trelawney?'

Garron could only stall and shake his head. He wondered if Kit was listening, and what he might make of his ex-wife's intervention.

He didn't think Kit would favour Melissa's ideas for a playground full of heavy equipment any more than he and Gary did. Truthfully, it was getting harder and harder to work out what everybody wanted.

Fortunately, at that moment, the band struck a booming note and the reporter spoke excitedly into her microphone.

'One moment, listeners! As I think you may be able to hear, the Penarren festival proper is about to get under-way . . . '

The band wheeled right, and all at once the crowd near Garron were laughing, smiling and waving. He heaved a sigh of relief; it would be impossible to answer any more questions. He smiled and clapped with the others to the beat of the music.

To a rousing blast of the tune 'One And All', Penarren's festival procession, with its hats, flags, candyfloss and shuffling feet, at last began to move along the beach road.

Misunderstandings

That evening, Jenny hurried down the back stairs at the Chough.

'Is my collar straight at the back?' she asked her daughter-in-law. It had been a rushed and busy day. She'd barely had time to find a top and skirt that matched, let alone climb into them tidily.

'Let me see . . . ' Kerensa patted the collar into place. 'There. That's fine. You off with Pauley Biddick, then?'

'Just for an hour or two,' Jenny said, collecting her new jacket from the hallstand in case the air felt cool on the way home. 'He thought it would be good to stand back from the festival hullaballoo for a little while!'

'Don't know where you get the energy,' Kerensa said with a yawn.

Jenny halted in the doorway, one hand on the door handle.

'You make sure you put your feet up now, Kerensa Hawke!' she said with mock severity. 'You've worked hard today and pregnant ladies need their rest!'

Kerensa smiled and nodded, easing her back with one hand.

Paul greeted Jenny outside with a longer hug than usual.

'Car's just round the corner,' he told her.

'I thought we were walking up to the Merrymaid,' Jenny said in surprise.

'That's not where we're heading . . . ' Paul said enigmatically.

They drove slowly past the pub and out of a still-crowded and festive Penarren until they reached a low, grey building a mile or two along the inland road. The sea appeared far off as a smoky blue-grey line between the hills. Paul drove into the tiny car park, and smiled at Jenny.

'I thought we'd try here for a change.'

Getting out of the car, Jenny felt

another twinge of worry. This wasn't their usual sort of place at all.

'Any particular reason?' she asked.

'I thought we deserved time out. Penarren's been like a hothouse!'

'You're right!' Jenny said with feeling. 'My feet haven't touched the ground for weeks . . . '

★   ★   ★

The restaurant was much as it had been when Dan had brought her here, years before. The same low ceilings and heavy beams, the same small, dark windows with their pretty floral curtains. The tables were different, though. They used to be bigger. Now they were small and square, with only enough room for two at each one.

Paul led the way across the soft carpet to a quiet corner table beside a window.

'My treat . . . ' he said with a smile, pulling out a chair for her.

Jenny hesitated.

'I . . . I'd rather share as we usually do, Paul . . . if you don't mind.'

He looked suddenly crestfallen.

'You know what I mean,' she said, feeling unaccountably guilty.

Paul smiled gently.

'Reckon I do,' he said. 'You're saying: cool it. That's OK. I can do cool if I have to.'

'I don't want to spoil the evening,' Jenny said.

'I was hoping . . . perhaps we might make this a less . . . um . . . predictable evening than usual,' Paul replied, slightly discomfited.

There was a pause while a waiter took their order. Jenny seized the opportunity to direct the conversation down another path.

'I had to put our friend Kit right on a misunderstanding earlier today,' she said.

'Kit isn't usually one to get the wrong end of the stick. What happened?' Paul asked.

'Apparently, he heard a news item on

local radio this morning about the Chough, followed by the reporter saying that Penarreners would do their utmost to stop Vennings damaging the eco-system.'

'Where did they get that from?'

'They interviewed my dad down by the harbour about the festival. Except Kit only caught snippets and must have thought they were quoting me!'

'So what did you say?'

'That he couldn't have been listening properly. That while I wouldn't have said the same thing as my father, retired coxswains had a perfect right to answer however they liked! Kit was upset, but he had the grace to apologise once he'd realised he'd got it wrong.'

Paul frowned.

'Well, you know Mum and I have never agreed with his plans, either. But as time goes on . . . I don't know if I'd still agree with everything the opposition says. After all, those old places by the harbour have been put to good use for the first time since I can remember.

I might begin to change my mind!'

He sighed.

'I'm not usually one for changing, as you know, but sometimes, Jenny, it can be a good thing, don't you think?'

Jenny hesitated. She wasn't sure she wanted to hear what Paul might say next.

'You can count on me to like you just the way you are!' she said with a smile, hoping to lighten the mood.

Paul frowned again.

Despite Jenny's best efforts, by the time the coffee arrived he'd steered their discussion into very serious waters.

You and Me — Together

'Jenny, listen to what I'm really saying. You know how well we get along . . . '

'And I'm sure we always will,' she replied.

Paul reached for her hand and held it.

'These days I'm thinking more about the future . . . and I think we should get together more often.'

'Like when you kissed me, on the beach that time?'

'Like when we kissed, Jenny. You and me together . . . that's how I want us to be.'

Painfully, Jenny recalled that even then the Chough had been as much in her mind as Paul. And since that time she hadn't felt the stirrings of romance, while he clearly had. But how could she break it to him? She needed to be straightforward with her friend, but she couldn't bear to hurt his feelings.

'I don't think you meant 'less predictable' earlier, did you, Pauley Biddick?' she said gently. 'You meant 'more romantically involved'.'

'I'd really like that to happen, Jenny, if you felt the same, of course. You know I would!'

She felt his hands warmly enclosing hers.

'I'm so sorry,' Jenny said, after the silence between them had stretched to snapping point. 'It isn't that I don't care for you — of course I do! But romance . . . love . . . '

He only clasped her hands more tightly.

'Why not?' he insisted. 'Is it because of Dan?'

Jenny shook her head.

'Dan was your best friend and my husband, and I loved him deeply. But he died a long time ago and I had to move on. I can't honestly say it's because I'm tied to the past . . . '

'So why do you think we can't have a future?'

'All I know is I never want to stop being friends, Paul. But if you want more . . . then I think it's not me you're looking for.'

He allowed her hands to slip from his.

'I'm sorry. I never thought to ask before, but . . . is there . . . someone else?'

Jenny shook her head again.

'Still friends, then, I hope?' Paul asked quietly.

'Always,' Jenny confirmed.

Still Friends

They walked separately towards the car and drove home in thoughtful silence. Jenny's relief that they had managed to talk so plainly was overshadowed by her concern about Paul and whether they really would be able to stay friends.

She watched the summer fairy lights, festooned around the door of the Merrymaid in honour of the festival, glimmer brightly as they slid past in the car.

'I'm sorry I can't persuade you we'd be good together,' Paul said. 'But best to have it out in the open now, I suppose. At least there's less hurt that way. And . . . despite everything . . . I want you to know I'm glad we're still friends.'

He hugged her as usual when they parted. Jenny sensed he might still have offered more than a peck on her cheek, had she not rested one hand on his shoulder and eased herself away.

'Thanks for a lovely evening,' she whispered. 'It was good to take a break from things here for a while.'

'Any time, sweetheart,' he murmured. 'Any time.'

And then he left, walking steadily across the shadowed pavement beside her café. She watched her friend anxiously, glad to see how he squared his shoulders as he reached the kerb. Jenny managed a smile. Nothing kept a lifeboatman down for long.

★　★　★

'Here you are, Mum!' Bea said, holding out a glass of orange juice. 'You look as if you could do with this!'

Melissa dabbed the back of one wrist delicately across her forehead, and accepted the cool drink with her free hand.

'Thank you, Beatrice.'

'Sit down for a while,' Bea suggested,

bumping a folding chair across the firm sand behind Melissa's tombola stall. 'I'll see to any customers.'

'I think I'll take your advice. My feet are aching!' Melissa sank into the seat with a huge sigh.

Despite the thronging hubbub around her, she soon felt refreshed, focusing on the white curl of the waves far out in the cove while she sipped her drink.

'I haven't worked as hard as this since . . . well, since I first became your father's secretary!' Melissa said.

Bea laughed.

'I can imagine, Mum! Dad still works hard, but perhaps not all the hours he used to. He's mellowed a bit!'

Melissa turned to smile at her daughter.

'You're right! Recently, we've been able to discuss everything — including you, Beatrice — far more easily than we used to.'

'It's been great you could stay and help him, Mum,' Bea said.

'Just remind me, for the sake of my

aching back, what else made me get roped into these Penarren festival activities!' Melissa said with a wry smile.

Bea grinned.

'Because you love to get compliments! Will Gulliver says you're a natural when it comes to organising.'

'Will's a nice man,' Melissa murmured.

'You've taken some of the load off Sophie, too,' Bea went on. 'I reckon that's made these past few weeks easier for both of them.'

'Poor Sophie . . . ' Melissa said.

'What makes you say that?' Bea asked.

'So far from home, with a small baby to take care of — it can't be easy. I was never keen on the idea myself . . . '

'But, Mum! This is her home!'

Melissa shook her head.

'I don't think Sophie Gulliver sees it that way, Beatrice. Perhaps that's why we get along so well. I've never felt entirely at home here, either. That's why I hardly ever came here with your father.'

'But you've got stuck in this time!' Bea observed.

'I know this sounds odd, but I felt I owed your father some support. It's a project close to his heart and yours, too, Beatrice, if I'm not mistaken. I just wish Derek had felt able to stay . . . '

Melissa privately wished she could stop missing her fiancé so much, but, self-contained as ever, would never say so.

'At least it's kept me busy!' she said brightly.

'Even Daveth's been warning me not to let you exhaust yourself,' Bea said.

Melissa sipped the last of her drink and stood up, brushing her immaculate jeans. She straightened her smartly tailored shirt and tucked a gold necklet into place.

'I'm sure Daveth's very kind,' Melissa said, a slight coolness creeping into her tone.

'Daveth's just concerned, Mum,' Bea

said, handing out a prize to another happy winner.

'No need,' Melissa said briskly. Then she noticed her daughter's reaction and sighed. 'I'm sorry, Beatrice. It's just that you seem to quote Daveth's views on almost everything lately.'

'That's because he's my friend, Mum.'

Melissa read the ticket numbers for two customers and regained control of her stall.

'Not more important than all your other friends, surely, darling?' She was dismayed to see her daughter's expression. Daveth was a nice young man, but it was important for Beatrice to realise that she wouldn't be staying long enough in Penarren to build serious relationships.

'We mustn't forget your college plans, darling,' she said with a light touch on Bea's arm.

'If I do,' Bea said, with an oddly brittle smile that worried her mother, 'then you and Dad will be sure to remind me!'

Bea stepped away from the stall. Melissa knew she was looking for Daveth.

'Don't worry, Mum,' Bea said. 'I'll see you later . . . OK?'

Luck of The Draw

Melissa felt her heart sink as her daughter waved and disappeared among the press of people. Almost immediately she saw Daveth wave, too. He came into view, holding aloft a pink teddy bear he'd obviously won somewhere. Melissa saw him present it to the laughing girl and the couple moved on, hand in hand.

'Is it a pound a go here, or not?' someone asked, holding a coin towards Melissa over the tombola prizes.

'What? Oh ... sorry ... yes, of course!' Melissa hurried to take the payment, and rolled the tickets in the red-painted wooden drum. 'Please take your tickets. Anything with a five or a nought wins ... '

'It says fifty-six here!' said the man, holding out his ticket. 'Is that near enough?'

Melissa focused fully on her customer and sighed inwardly.

'I'm so sorry,' she said, politely examining the ticket and shaking her head. 'It must be exactly a five or a ten.'

'So it's no good?' the man said in a huff. 'I'm trying somewhere else!'

'Please, do . . . ' a polite voice suggested. A tall figure edged its way gently forward as the grumpy customer left. Melissa felt her heart stop.

'Derek?' She gasped.

'One tombola ticket, please!' Melissa's fiancé said. 'And then, if you could find someone to take over for a little while, I'd be honoured if the most beautiful woman on the beach would have lunch with me.'

Melissa put one hand to her throat. Her heart was racing.

'What . . . what are you doing here?' she asked, accepting his payment as if in a dream.

'Losing at least a pound on your tombola stall, I imagine!' Derek smiled.

'Is anything wrong?' Melissa asked anxiously.

'Nothing at all,' Derek reassured her.

'But you don't like Penarren, Derek!'

'True,' he agreed. 'All the same . . . I had to come . . . '

Melissa saw his soulful eyes level with hers, and her heart missed another beat. As she gave Derek his ticket, he caught her hand and wouldn't let it go.

'You see, my dear, I decided I really couldn't live without you. I'm so sorry we had . . . our slight disagreement. I've come to apologise. We need to talk . . . I don't want to go back to London again like this, it's been wretched.'

Trembling slightly, Melissa clasped Derek's hands. The people behind him in the queue were smiling.

'I owe you an apology, too,' she said. 'I'm so pleased to see you, Derek . . . you can't imagine how pleased . . . '

Tears began to spill unbidden down her cheeks. Derek whisked a spotless white handkerchief from his top pocket and hurried behind the stall.

'Now, now . . . please don't cry, my darling. I've given you a shock! Dry your eyes, and I'll stay and help you run the stall until Beatrice returns. She will be back fairly soon, I take it?'

Melissa, feeling foolish and very happy, dabbed her eyes with Derek's well-pressed handkerchief. It smelled sweetly of cologne.

'I'll get her on her mobile phone . . .'

She turned away and began dialling, but there was no reply.

'Keep trying,' Derek urged, now rolling up his sleeves behind the stall.

Melissa checked and dialled again, but Beatrice wasn't answering.

Pleasure Cruise

Further along the beach, Jenny, with Ben in her arms, shifted his weight on her hip as he wriggled impatiently.

'I want a ride on Baz's boat. Please, Nana.'

'Wouldn't you like to stay and watch Uncle Pauley on the *Etta*?' Jenny asked.

She pointed out the splendid gleam of the lifeboat as it rounded into the cove from beyond the harbour. It was Saturday, and the *Etta's* crew were providing the grand finale of the week-long festival.

Ben wriggled again, inadvertently tugging Jenny's hair, and she winced.

'Can we go on Baz's boat in a minute?' he asked earnestly.

'Are you sure it's going out today, Ben?'

Ben nodded.

'Daddy said.'

Jenny sighed and smiled. Ben was used to the lifeboat. Watching a demonstration was a bit more exciting, but she knew her grandson would far rather have something more active to do. Sometimes he reminded Jenny so much of Dan.

'All right, Ben. But first we must tell your daddy, and second you must promise to hold my hand all the time. Agreed?'

Ben slid to the ground, beaming.

'Yes!'

The *Etta* turned in a graceful arc across the cove, leaving a wake of creamy-white foam, but Jenny and Ben left the watching crowd behind. After telling Gary, they walked towards the harbour to buy a ticket to see the Chough rock.

The pleasure boat *Rosenwyn* was owned by the Trudgian brothers, the three sons of Fred and his wife Sue at the Merrymaid. The boys were all members of the lifeboat crew. Today, however, Baz and Mark were in charge of the family concern, and only Alan was taking part in the lifeboat demonstration.

'I'm holding you tight, aren't I, Nana?' Ben said, gripping Jenny's hand as they reached the harbour side. She smiled; he was trying hard to be good.

'You certainly are!' she said.

Their tickets were punched and they climbed aboard the *Rosenwyn*.

'Hello, there, young Ben!' Baz said, lifting the child on to the deck. 'Not watching the ol' *Etta*, then?'

'He wanted this last outing so badly,' Jenny said.

She searched the small deck for a space on one of the benches. Several tourists shuffled closer together and Ben squeezed in beside her.

Baz signalled the all-clear and cast off. The engine sputtered as Mark gently turned the wheel to steer them out of the harbour. Apart from Baz and Mark, Jenny realised she and Ben were the only Penarreners aboard.

'Super festival, isn't it?' the passenger

beside her said, a tall, grey-haired lady wearing a green headscarf. 'I can see your little boy loves it!' She patted Ben's curly head.

No Cause For Alarm

Mark guided the *Rosenwyn* as the little craft worked its way towards Penarren Head. The sun lit up the Chough rock.

It looked more hawk than chough from the seaward, Dan had often said. Dan had developed his early love of rock climbing near those cliffs. With his long, easy reach, he'd made everything look effortless. Jenny sighed as she held close the little grandson who so reminded her of his grandfather.

The *Rosenwyn* swung into the shelter of the headland.

'You can see the lifeboat from here, Ben!' she said.

Ben nodded, but for now he was intent on watching seagulls.

'Two entertainments for the price of one ticket,' the lady next to them put in. 'Now that's what I call value for money!'

It was as they moved close to the shelter of the cliffs that Jenny first felt the *Rosenwyn* shudder. It was the smallest hiccup, but instinctively she glanced towards the cabin. None of the other passengers seemed to have noticed.

When Mark winked at Ben, Jenny assumed all was well and turned her head again to watch the *Etta* now riding smoothly in the water. The display would be taking place in full view of the beach, but mostly out of sight of the pleasure boat. She could see two orange-clad figures on the deck, but from this distance she found it impossible to say who they were.

Ben gazed down, entranced by the water rushing past the boat. Jenny held him firmly. It was as well she did. Abruptly, the engine faded. Instead of rushing, the water gulped and lapped at the sides. There was a smell of hot oil. Jenny saw Baz Trudgian ease himself into a space beside the cabin and speak to his brother.

This time, the engine did not restart.

'No cause for alarm, ladies and gentlemen,' Baz announced through the on-board loudspeaker. 'We'll soon have her running . . . '

Ben grew tired of being held, and could not be deterred from sliding to the deck to trot across to his friend. Baz smiled, reached down and lifted the little boy in his arms. Concerned that he'd be in the way, Jenny hurried forward to reclaim her grandson.

'Mrs Hawke . . . ' Baz murmured, when she was near enough to hear. 'Looks like this might take a while . . . '

'Anything I can do?' Jenny asked softly.

'Show 'em some Penarraner calm,' Baz said with a smile. 'Worry is catching!'

Jenny slid back to her seat and settled Ben on her lap.

'What's wrong?' Jenny's neighbour asked.

'It's nothing to worry about,' Jenny assured her.

That much was true, but Jenny knew they were drifting. It was almost imperceptible just now, but if the boat didn't get underway in the next minute or two . . .

Jenny had lived in Penarren all her life, and was the daughter of the lifeboat coxswain. She'd grown up hearing all the tales about the dangers faced by seafarers caught in the strong currents beyond the mouth of the cove.

She continued to make conversation with her neighbours, but increasingly her mind drifted with the boat. She noticed others begin to shift in their seats, or crane their necks for a clearer view of the cabin. She took a deep breath and concentrated on keeping her expression calm.

Keeping Cheerful

'I'm hungry!' Ben announced, squirming on her lap.

Disregarding the rule about no sweets between meals, Jenny was glad of the distraction. She found a tube of fruit pastilles at the bottom of her bag, and gave one to Ben. She offered them round. Nobody else took one.

'I hope we'll be underway soon,' her neighbour said. 'I've got a coach to catch!'

'Won't be long now . . . ' Jenny said, hoping she was right.

The sun had left the Chough rock, and the breeze freshened. In another five minutes — possibly less — the *Rosenwyn* would be carried near Penarren Point. Beyond that rolled the open sea. Jenny felt her shoulders tighten. She gave Ben another sweet.

Baz Trudgian turned away, flicked a

switch and spoke briefly into a handset. There was a hiss of static, then a reply. He nodded to his brother and clapped him on the shoulder approvingly.

'Ladies and gentlemen.' Baz stepped forward. 'There is no cause for alarm . . . '

'What does he mean?' Her neighbour's voice, close to Jenny's ear and brimming with anxiety, prevented her hearing the rest of Baz's words.

'I think we're about to become part of a lifeboat demo,' Jenny said, determined to keep cheerful. Hitching her grandson close to her side, Jenny reached over and patted the woman's arm. She subsided, looking glum.

Danger Ahead

Baz moved slowly around the deck.

'Mark reckons he'll get her going; meanwhile, we've radioed in,' he said as he passed Jenny. 'Coastguard says someone else had already spotted us from the beach, wonder who it was?'

'I saw my dad on the beach. I'll bet it was him!' Jenny said, certain that Garron Trelawney would have noticed as soon as there was anything amiss at sea.

'I'd bet on that, too,' Baz agreed with a grin.

Among the mutter of voices and anxiously shared looks all around her, Jenny steadfastly kept her smile in place. She set her eye — and her hopes — on the distant outline of the *Etta Trelawney*, willing it at every moment to turn towards them. The sea was ruffled as if someone had breathed on it. Beneath that troubled surface, dark swirls of brooding green and purple waters came and went.

With every passing moment, the Trudgians' little pleasure boat bobbed and swung in the currents progressing inexorably, wave by wave, towards the mouth of the cove . . .

Rescue

'What you gone and done with our ol' boat, m'handsome?' Baz Trudgian's young brother called. Alan Trudgian grinned as he leaned over the rail of the *Etta Trelawney*. 'You'll have some explaining to do to our dad, and no mistake!'

By this time, the Penarren lifeboat crew had secured a line to a cleat aboard the *Rosenwyn* and their coxswain judged the leisure-boat passengers safe. They'd stay on board to be towed.

Baz gave the thumbs-up.

Jenny saw Kit leaning on the rail next to Fred Trudgian's youngest. Ben spotted him, too, and waved. Kit waved back.

A subdued but heartfelt cheer came from the *Rosenwyn*'s passengers as they got underway.

Steadily, the *Etta* moved ahead to

meet the waves and give what shelter it could to the smaller boat.

'It's a mite choppier in open water,' Jenny's neighbour muttered, refastening her green headscarf.

Jenny felt Ben's arms tighten around her neck as the leisure craft met the swell in its turn. She murmured in his ear promises of his favourite baked beans for supper, but her grandson looked more excited than frightened. They watched the boats' uneven rise and fall, and the strong rope between them alternately tugging and dipping.

Jenny kept her eyes on Kit. To her horror she saw him leave the lifeboat's rail just as a strong cross-wave caught the *Etta* side on. She could only watch helplessly when Kit mis-timed his only chance to steady himself and the deck plummeted beneath his feet.

Afterwards, Jenny thought if only he'd held the rail a moment longer, or if the sea hadn't rolled — any one of a hundred possibilities — the accident would never have happened. But all she could do now was listen to the pounding of her heart.

Kit, flung clear by the unpredictable movement, dropped beside the lifeboat like an orange rag. The splash as he hit the water sent up a starburst of white foam, quickly swallowed in the swell. Jenny stared at the spot among the waves where Kit had disappeared and only breathed out when she caught sight of his headgear. Shouts carried on the air and all around her. A flurry of well-drilled activity, and Paul and the others were soon hauling their crew-mate aboard. But Kit didn't move as he reached the deck.

Her arms tightly gripping Ben, mouth dry and heart racing, Jenny couldn't see what happened next. That uncertainty was worse than anything.

Sleepless Night

Next morning, Jenny pushed open the door of Kit's hospital room. A waft of disinfectant caught her throat. Kit lay in a high bed, his face still and pale, his eyes shut. Although Garron had travelled with Kit in the ambulance and had brought reassurances home to the Chough the previous evening, Jenny had spent a sleepless night.

She moved a chair closer to Kit's bedside and sat down.

He opened his eyes.

'Jenny.'

At first, he could manage only her name, and her hands tightened anxiously on the edge of her seat. Kit swallowed.

'Thanks . . . I asked Mel to ask you . . . glad you could come. Sorry about everything . . . '

Jenny had a flashback of that dreadful

moment when she'd seen Kit's orange-clad shape hauled slowly up the dark blue side of the rolling *Etta*.

'You poor love!' she said, the words tight in her throat.

'The crew were great . . . ' Kit managed. 'Got me out quickly.'

Jenny was relieved to hear his voice becoming stronger, but his speech was slow. Still the effects of last night's sedation, she supposed. Without thinking, she slipped her hand around his, her thumb moving gently across the soft skin beneath his wrist, offering what comfort she could.

'How's the leg?' she asked.

'Hurts a bit,' Kit muttered.

His brows were drawn in a small frown. He looked as he had long ago, the only child of parents who kept themselves and their young son aloof. Jenny blinked back tears. Dan and Paul had been his best friends then, but he'd often been prevented from seeing them.

It was a jolt to Jenny, realising how close she had become to Kit Venning, someone she'd never anticipated seeing again after he'd left Penarren all those years ago. She'd argued, discussed, disagreed and wrangled with this man over village matters for months, and she supposed they'd become friends. But it wasn't friendship she felt this morning. This was something she'd once felt for Dan but never for anyone since.

'Lily sent cakes . . . ' Kit said, his hand moving over hers.

Jenny followed his glance towards a flowery tin on the locker.

'Anything Lily bakes is a well-known cure,' she said tenderly.

'Promise me you'll eat them all.'

Kit managed a half-smile.

'For you?' Anything,' he said. 'Your hair's so pretty this morning . . . ' he added. He focused his gaze on her.

'I'm so worried, Jenny . . . this accident would happen just as the riverside project is getting underway.'

'Don't fret,' she soothed.

'I must get home.' Kit freed anxious fingers and Jenny reached quickly across the bed to hold them again.

'Give yourself time,' she said, patting his hand.

'Mel and Derek . . . very kind . . . but they don't know the building schedule.'

'Melissa gave me a key to the office, Kit. Don't worry.'

She returned to stroking his arm, to calm herself as much as him. She shared some of his worries. Soon Melissa would marry Derek, and Kit would be alone. As for Mel and Kit's wilful beautiful daughter . . .

'Bea's with young Daveth,' Kit said, chiming in with Jenny's thoughts. 'Nice lad, but bad timing. I encouraged her to live here, but now . . . I'm not sure I did the right thing . . .'

Jenny gently lifted his hand and held it against her cheek. How thunderously that simple action made her heart beat!

'Remember, whatever happens, I'll always be here. For both of you,' she whispered.

His gaze met hers steady and intense. 'There's no-one we — I — need more than you, Jenny, my love.'

His fingers stroked her cheek. Impulsively she turned to kiss them.

'You look worn out. Perhaps I should go.'

'Please stay . . . ' he said. 'I miss you when we're apart . . . '

So Jenny stayed, one side of her face pressed against his palm.

When he slept, she settled his arm on the coverlet and stood up.

She hadn't felt this way about him before, but then she'd never heard him so . . . so unguarded before. Stretched to his considerable length in the bed, his feet had pushed up the end of the blankets. She re-folded them, and then waited to be sure he still slept.

At last, brushing at tears she'd been holding back, she gave a deep sigh and left.

A Good Team

'Catch hold, Bea!' Daveth called.

Beatrice grasped Daveth Rosewarne's fingers and half-jumped, half-scrambled beside him on the steeply sloping grass.

'What d'you reckon?' he asked smiling.

'Great!' Bea said. She shaded her eyes as the evening sunshine floated on to a calm sea from beneath the clouds. Bea felt she was floating, too, basking in Daveth's gaze.

'See any seagulls?'

'Tons!' Bea answered, spreading her arms.

'It must be handsome to hover above water like that . . .'

'Mmm,' Bea agreed happily, tilting her face to the glow.

Daveth leaned forward to kiss her cheek.

'That's my girl!' he said. 'It's good to

have you more cheerful.'

'My poor dad . . . ' Bea said, drawing in her arms and wrapping them close around her body. 'He looked so helpless, I could hardly bear it. Yet he kept on and on about his wretched plans! I told him Mum was on the case!'

Daveth hugged Bea to his side.

'Your dad's had no choice but to let things slide a bit. I'm glad he's improving. He's in good hands at home. Perhaps I shouldn't say this . . . but is your mum always such a force of nature?'

Bea giggled.

'Bossy? Oh yes! Usually she's much worse! I think maybe she's eased up just lately, now Dad's stronger. Derek's doing his best, too, but he must get fed up being told what to do!'

Daveth shook his head.

'Actually, I think he and your mum make a good team. Derek speaks his mind.'

Bea considered this. Perhaps she

might get used to her mum being married to someone else. Maybe Derek wasn't so bad, after all. Daveth always saw things positively. It was what Bea loved about him.

Helping Hand

They walked on, finally reaching the ancient church at the top of the valley.

They scrambled past, and on over the rough ground. Whenever she stumbled, Daveth's hand was there.

Bea felt the mild Cornish air pat her face and the tufts of grass spring under her feet. She wondered if she'd ever feel happier than she did at this moment.

'When I go to London for Mum and Derek's wedding, will you miss me?' Bea asked.

'Of course,' Daveth said.

'Come with me, then!' she cried, catching his arm.

'I didn't get an invite,' Daveth joked. 'Anyway, I'm a newcomer on your scene,' he added more seriously. 'It wouldn't feel right.'

'It says on my invitation *Miss Beatrice Lucy Venning and guest*. You could be my guest.'

'Isn't your dad going with you?'

'He was going to sleep over a couple of nights at the London flat, then bring me back to Penarren at the end of the week. And now, even though I'll have to do all the driving because of this accident, he won't give up! I think he sees it as showing his support for Mum and Derek on their big day . . .

'I told him I was quite big enough to go to a wedding on my own, but Dad said he'd promised me and my mum, and no way was he going to let anyone down.'

In spite of her brave words, Bea was dearly hoping for her dad's company. Watching her mum getting married to someone new wasn't going to be easy, and she wanted Kit around. Bea sighed and frowned.

'No, not that way, Bea! Come over here,' Daveth called.

He was already measuring the ground in great, strong strides. Bea ran to catch up.

'What is it?' she demanded breath-lessly.

Daveth took her hand. The bushes and small trees clung thickly to the valley's side here, and Bea found herself gazing into a slight hollow. Leaves and branches whispered overhead.

Enchantment

A low granite arch enclosed a black, unexpected pool. White flowers gleamed in the grass nearby. It was so quiet Bea could scarcely hear the beat of the waves.

'What is it?' Bea felt she ought to whisper.

'A well. The sort everyone used to know about, but now everyone seems to have forgotten.' Daveth smiled his wide, charming smile. That smile had been working its magic on Bea ever since she'd met him. She stepped away from the stone edge of the fathomless circle of water and leaned against him.

'What are you thinking?' Daveth asked quietly, slipping an arm around Bea's waist to steady her.

'That I want to be wherever you are all the time,' she said. 'Come to London with me, Daveth. No-one will mind . . .'

When he didn't answer, Bea twisted in his arms and gazed at him.

'Please . . . ' she said, in the tone that always won over her father.

Smiling, Daveth smoothed Bea's hair and held her head gently between his hands.

'Bea, we've already discussed this, and you know how impossible it is for me to take time off work at short notice.'

'But why shouldn't we be happy and together like this for always?' Bea demanded.

'I think you might need some time on your own, or perhaps with your dad. Just to see you safely back next week will be fine by me,' Daveth said. His voice was light, but he looked more serious than Bea had ever seen him.

'But it'll be awful leaving you, and everyone, even for one week. I'm sure you don't realise how much I'm going to miss you, Daveth, or you'd come with me. You would!'

Bea studied Daveth's face intently. At

last, she recognised he wasn't the kind of man likely to change his mind. She wound her arms tightly around his neck before they kissed.

No Parking!

An overloaded red lorry slowed at the foot of the hill and turned its huge black wheels into the car park beside the Chough. Paul Biddick, walking past after an early meeting with Baz Trudgian up at the Merrymaid, looked on curiously. The lorry's brakes groaned and gave out a monstrous hiss. Paul wondered if Jenny was expecting it.

His question was answered a second later when a door flew open and Jenny rushed down the steps, looking decidedly flustered with hair and pink overall askew. Unwilling to leave this particular damsel in distress, Paul strolled over.

'Looks like another delivery for Vennings,' he said as he approached.

'Nobody mentioned it to me!' Jenny called over her shoulder. 'They've been up and down to the riverside site for weeks, but they take the bigger loads via the cove, thank goodness.'

'Perhaps you'd best ring Vennings, then?'

'Kit isn't there. He declared himself well enough to travel with Bea for Melissa and Derek's wedding!' Jenny said.

'Surely someone must know,' Paul muttered.

'You can't park here!' Jenny told the lorry driver as he clambered from his cab.

'Car parking is for Chough customers only,' Paul emphasised.

The driver scratched the back of his head.

'I have to leave this lot somewhere . . . ' he said.

'Not here,' Paul interrupted.

'It's OK, Paul,' Jenny said. 'I can see to this.'

She planted her hands on her hips and fixed the lorry driver with a look Paul knew well.

'Nobody ordered this,' Jenny asserted.

'Someone did,' the driver said,

looking pained. 'Foundations for hard-standing. They told us up-along there was a sort of a playground getting built down by the river, so we followed that direction.'

'But it's a conservation area!' Paul said.

'You can't reach the site from here unless you go on foot,' Jenny said. 'You're not planning to take this load down one sackful at a time, are you?'

The driver grinned disarmingly, and indicated the load.

'No fear! We'd need a fair-sized wheelbarrow!'

Paul scanned the yellow lettering on the lorry's side and tailgate. It had come from a firm he'd never heard of some way inland.

'Shall I get your dad?' he asked.

'I don't think we need to bother Dad ... ' Jenny began, pushing distractedly at her fringe with the back of her wrist.

'Too late!' Paul said cheerily. 'Cox-swain's already on deck.'

Marching Orders

'How long is this lorry staying?' Garron demanded, standing beside Jenny.

'I'll only be here temporary . . . ' the driver replied.

'A likely tale,' Garron said.

'Mrs Hawke shouldn't have to deal with this upheaval at all!' Paul added, jabbing the air angrily with his finger.

'Take it easy, Paul.' Jenny sighed. She turned to the lorry driver. 'May I see the order sheet, please?'

The lorry driver rummaged inside his cab and finally located a much-folded paper.

'Thanks,' Jenny said, and read it.

'What's it say?' Garron asked over his daughter's shoulder.

'It's the sort of rubble Kit promised Gary he'd avoid using in such a sensitive coastal area,' Jenny said.

'What does Kit think he's doing?'

Paul demanded.

Jenny read on, her forehead creased with anxiety. Then she let out a huge sigh.

'Thank goodness . . . this delivery is for Vanson's, not Vennings!' she said. 'The writing's got smudged.'

Paul glanced down the delivery sheet.

'You'll have to head back towards Bodmin to deliver,' he told the driver. He patted Jenny reassuringly on the shoulder. How lucky he'd been on hand to help.

Then, just as the driver finished telephoning for clearer instructions, the tailgate clicked. Almost simultaneously, it shrugged out a landslip of stones. The heap deposited itself, pyramid-fashion, on the tarmac in a cloud of dust.

Coughing and spluttering, the little group was forced to step back.

'That'll take a while to shift, for certain,' the driver said ruefully. 'Anyone got an extra shovel?'

There was a tense pause.

'I'll do it,' Paul said grimly. 'But only on account of the Chough, mind!'

Blameless

Jenny opened her café a little later than usual. Paul accepted Garron's offer of coffee. He shook his head at the responses of father and daughter. Jenny had managed to see the funny side. Garron hadn't been quite so successful.

'That's put paid to business!' Garron grumbled. 'Who wants to walk past a dusty ol' rubble lorry?'

'It'll be going in a minute,' Jenny reassured him.

'As if we hadn't enough upheaval with Kit's schemes around the village already!' Paul put in.

'I'm having a word with that Kitto when he gets back,' Garron said as he went to set up the coffee machine. 'Whether his leg's better or no!'

'I fail to see how this morning's bother has anything to do with a man at this moment blamelessly hobbling around

London on a pair of crutches!' Jenny called, mixing a batch of scones in a flurry of flour.

'The one thing Kit doesn't need,' Paul said in exasperation, his arms still aching from his shovelling efforts, 'is you or anyone else to stick up for him, Jenny.'

While he wanted his crewmate to get better quickly, Paul didn't feel Kit and his building schemes deserved to get off lightly. Then, seeing Jenny's crestfallen face, Paul grinned and changed tack.

'Anyway, thanks for the coffee, my special sweetheart!' he said, swamping her in his usual bear-hug. He landed a noisy kiss on her cheek to which Jenny retaliated by dusting his face with flour. Still chuckling, Paul followed Garron into the café.

'I doubt that lorry driver would ever have come this way if rumours about building down-along hadn't been so well known,' Paul said to Garron, once out of Jenny's hearing.

'I'm glad someone sees things from

my point of view,' Garron muttered.

'I wonder sometimes why Jenny supports Kit so much,' Paul said. 'Reckon it's time we all got back to normal around here!'

'She was all for co-operating with him from the start. Don't forget they've been meeting pretty regular since he came back to Trenfos.'

'Meeting? How often?'

'Every week or so . . . it seems more often since young Kitto's accident, now I think of it. Well, we all wanted to help him then, of course! But me and Lily Pinch have had to cover for her at the café when she's up Trenfos, keeping the accounts or whatever she's been doing for Kit while he's away. Lately I swear she's never where she belongs!'

Paul paid for a biscuit from the counter, unwrapped it and bit into it thoughtfully.

'You and Kit's dad, old Mr Venning, you didn't see things the same, so I've heard,' Paul began.

Garron eased the back of his neck

with one hand. He frowned.

'I've tried real hard not to let past history affect my dealings with Kit Venning, Pauley. I owe the cheel that much.'

Paul brushed the biscuit crumbs from his jacket. He didn't know the whole story, after all.

'Must be tricky for you,' Garron continued sympathetically. 'Like me, you'd always want to be on friendly terms with a crewmate.'

Paul left the Chough, moodily wondering how much longer that state of affairs was likely to last.

Welcome Home

Trenfos house was bright with late summer afternoon sunshine. Jenny sat in Kit's office recording the mistaken delivery in case of further dispute, and other more routine events in the schedule during the past week.

Kit had rung the previous evening to say when he and Bea would be back, so Jenny had brought some groceries to welcome them home.

Absorbed in work, Jenny heard the door slam before she realised Kit and his daughter had arrived. Dropping papers into a pile, she hurried to the hall.

'Welcome home!' she greeted them. 'How was your journey?'

'Dad's tired,' Bea said, pulling a face.

Kit, still using crutches, shuffled forward.

'I told you — I'm fine!' he said.

'I'll make us all a hot drink,' Jenny offered.

'Thank you.' Kit swung himself through the office doorway.

Weary Traveller

Jenny spotted him peering at the papers she'd just abandoned. In the hall, Bea gave a small shrug before disappearing upstairs with her luggage.

'He takes no notice of me . . . ' she told Jenny in a low voice as she passed.

'So — how was London?' Jenny asked as she carried in the tray.

'The wedding?' Kit's gaze was still fixed on the desk. 'Bea enjoyed herself, I think. Mel looked wonderful, of course. Derek was OK, but a bit nervous.'

'And . . . you?'

'Fine, honestly,' he answered. 'I could see how happy Mel was . . . I was only there to wish the couple well before they left, really. Didn't want to be the spectre at the feast!'

'Is that how you feel, then? Ghost-like?'

Kit looked up.

'What's my daughter been telling you?' he asked.

'Nothing. I just thought the journey might have tired you more than you admitted, that's all,' Jenny said.

Kit limped across the room to lower himself on to one of the seats in the bay window. Jenny joined him with the tea. The door opened behind her.

'Bea!' Jenny said. 'Would you like a cup?'

'My daughter looks all set to go out again right now, if you ask me!' Kit remarked.

Bea looked anxiously at her father.

'I won't stay . . . if you're sure you're all right, Dad,' she said, coming close. Kit accepted the kiss she dropped on his head, and then waved her towards the door.

'Don't fuss! I know you want to catch up with your friends.'

Bea left with a dazzling smile and a promise not to be late.

'She's off to meet Daveth Rosewarne.'

Kit sighed. 'I don't have the heart to stop her, even supposing I could!

'The last thing Mel said was, 'Make sure our daughter makes the right decision about college, Kitto. No woman should be without qualifications these days.' I agree with her. But how do I convince Bea?'

'Does it have to be either Daveth or studying?' Jenny mused. 'Is the choice so cut and dried these days?'

'Not really, if the young couple themselves can cope. It sounds awful to say this, but at the moment we're not convinced Bea's mature enough to deal with so much change at once.'

'Perhaps you could sell Bea on the idea of independence first?'

'But you know how happy she's been this summer, Jenny . . . I dread having to wrench her away from Trenfos and Daveth just when she's learned to love them both.'

Crisis of Confidence

Kit got up and leaned heavily on his crutches. 'Jenny, I'm sorry — I've been tetchy since we got inside the front door,' he said at last.

Jenny smiled forgiveness and continued to move around the sitting room, tidying as she went.

'You don't have to,' Kit said, watching her. 'Mrs Pethick will be in tomorrow.'

Jenny lifted cups on to the tray and wiped the low table underneath.

'Force of habit.' She grinned.

She saw Kit's shoulders relax.

'Where are my manners?' he exclaimed. 'You've been so kind. Looking in on the house for me, keeping up the accounts, not to mention the groceries today.'

'Including another cake from Lily! Morwenna Biddick sent you a dozen eggs, too, not to be outdone. You know you can't be in any sort of trouble in

Penarren and not have half the village competing to offer help . . . especially if you're a handsome lifeboatman injured in the line of duty . . . '

She was doing her best to lift him out of his dark mood, but Kit looked uncomfortable.

'The way I'm feeling, a lifeboatman's something I might not be for much longer,' he muttered.

Jenny put the half-filled tray on the arm of the settee and pushed at some cushions.

'I don't believe that!'

'It's true,' Kit said flatly. 'Far worse than the damage to my pride is the constant feeling I let everyone down.'

'It was an accident, Kit. Anyone on the *Etta* will tell you training takes time. Even more, finding your limits. I'll bet most of the crew would tell you they've been through a crisis of confidence more than once.'

Kit leaned on the back of the settee. His usually open face wore a pinched expression.

'Lily used to say when I was a boy my ideas ran away with me,' he said.

'What's that got to do with it?' Jenny demanded.

'I look at it this way. I came back to Penarren full of ideas I knew would change other people's lives,' Kit said. 'Joining the *Etta* at the same time seemed good, but a side-show by comparison. A boost to my image, perhaps! But you know what? Becoming part of that crew turned out to be the most important thing of all. I thought I was changing others' lives. Instead, it's mine that's changed the most.'

Let Me Help

One of Kit's crutches crashed to the floor and he couldn't reach it. He pressed one hand wearily across his eyes.

'You must be tired, whatever you say. Sit down,' Jenny urged. She ignored the crutch, but moved close to offer her arm. Kit rested his hand on her shoulder.

'Did I tell you what your dad said to me on the way to the hospital the night we towed the *Rosenwyn* in?' he asked. Jenny shook her head.

'He said: 'Never forget your crewmates think of you as close family. They'll want you back'.' Kit swallowed. 'Family was both the kindest and the most painful word he could have used . . . '

'Why?'

'Because at that moment I felt so

adrift from the crew . . . and from my daughter. From both my families, you might say.

'Your dad's words brought back other, more painful, memories, too. I'm sure I don't have to spell out those memories for a Trelawney . . . '

There had been rumours of friction between the Trelawney and Venning families in the past, but Jenny had dismissed them.

'My dad wasn't an easy man, Jenny,' Kit said, staring at the carpet. 'He spoke hastily, and held your father responsible for the effects of a near-disastrous rescue — bringing in a craft much like the *Rosenwyn*, as it happens. My mother was aboard.'

Jenny remembered.

'Dad came home saying he hoped he wouldn't have to answer a shout like it ever again. Panic's the worst thing.'

Kit nodded.

'I don't think my father understood that, however traumatic the rescue, real disaster was avoided because of the coxswain's judgement and the crew's bravery. He blamed my mother's later illness on the stress of the event.

'My mother couldn't bear to stay near the sea after that, so we moved to London. But I know my dad always, always wanted to come home.'

'Poor man,' Jenny said softly.

Kit pushed one hand through his hair.

'It's only now that I realise my motive for joining the lifeboat crew was selfish,' he said. 'It was as if I felt it could make up for the past!'

'Does that matter? The crew think you're doing a good job, Kit . . . and you can never know who you might help in the future.'

'I'm doubting all my motives lately. Perhaps I should never have returned to Penarren at all.'

'I hope you don't mean that!' Jenny said.

'You were managing very well before I came,' Kit pointed out. 'Perhaps it's just time to let things return to normal.'

'You're not thinking of abandoning our last project, are you?'

'Why not?' he said. 'There's hardly anyone who'd be disappointed.'

'Except me. And that project's the most important to you, too. You told me so yourself!'

'It was . . . until I realised most of the opposition to it comes from within your own family!'

★ ★ ★

Jenny bit her lip.

She'd managed to maintain her support for Kit's riverside scheme without losing the respect of either her father or her son. But that might change if the Chough couldn't pay its bills. So far, she'd confessed to no-one that the café could be heading for financial trouble.

'We usually shed our differences when we hang up our coats in the hall,' she said, struggling to sound optimistic. 'I don't want to cause bad feeling between our families again, if . . . '

'If what?'

Kit sighed.

'If the Chough is suffering, Jenny. Forgive me, but from your expression I'd say it's been happening for a while.'

Jenny turned away and sank on to the settee. She couldn't fool Kit.

'I meant to tell you,' she said. 'But I couldn't . . . not while you were still hobbling about on those crutches . . . '

She rubbed her face with both hands, and looked up.

'I haven't been too clever at the Chough, starting expensive work on the terrace. The café *is* struggling, but honestly we've been in this situation so often it's almost normal. Penarren's Patchwork Palace, my dad calls it!' She smiled ruefully.

Kit lowered himself beside Jenny and eased his injured leg into position.

'If only you'd let me help . . . '

Jenny felt she'd swallowed a dry pebble.

'Perhaps you should wait until you

can buy me out for the cost of a Cornish fairing,' she said at last. 'At least there'd be some business sense in that decision . . . '

Kit slid his arm across her shoulders.

'Business be blowed,' he murmured. 'After all that's happened, you know you mean more to me than that . . . '

Jenny leaned her head against him.

'I hope I didn't embarrass you at the hospital,' Kit said quietly. 'My mind wasn't that clear when we talked. But I want you to know I was awake enough to mean every word.'

'You said nothing I didn't want to hear,' Jenny said, her voice suddenly a little shaky. Her heart gave an untimed beat, but this time she welcomed it. She lifted her face to Kit's and smiled into his eyes.

'I meant all I said, too.'

Kit murmured something indistinct in reply. Then, as natural as a homecoming, he drew her close and Jenny felt the warmth of his lips on hers.

She brought her hand to rest against

his face and returned his deepening kiss. In the joyful rush of feelings, every past worry and every calculation for the future vanished from Jenny's mind like soft mist along the shore.

Divided Loyalties

'Ben! Be a good boy, now. Come and get dressed . . . ' Kerensa sounded tired. Jenny, preparing the lunchtime sandwiches in the Chough kitchen, hoped she and Gary wouldn't have to wait long for their new baby to arrive.

Jenny hoped it wouldn't be too long, either, before she could claim some of Kit's precious time. It had been hard to put him out of her mind after *that* kiss after his return from London.

Since then, the most intimate conversation they'd managed had been a warm smile and a quiet hello across the counter at lunchtimes. They had arranged a date one evening, but at the last minute Kit had been called away.

Shouts, and the clatter of a van unloading in the car park below the café, jolted Jenny back to the present and the imminent arrival of workmen to continue their work renovating the terrace. They saluted her through the window. She was just waving back when Garron stormed into the kitchen.

'Have you seen these?' he demanded. He thrust a handful of brown envelopes into view.

'Bills.' Jenny glanced down. 'Yes, Dad, I've seen them.'

'Well, I hadn't!'

'They were in the usual file,' Jenny said. 'Is there a problem?'

'There is if we haven't paid them yet, my girl. They're due this Friday!'

'We can pay, Dad.'

'For this month, maybe,' Garron said. 'But I checked the books after our last delivery. It won't be looking so good from next month. We both know the café's less busy at this end of the season.' Garron's glance took in the workmen, now hauling up their tools, and beyond them the new paving slabs stacked on the freshly sanded terrace.

'But we're no less busy rebuilding, it seems,' he said heavily.

'We agreed the terrace would be an investment in our future, didn't we?' Jenny asked.

'It would have been cheaper if I'd done it, Jenny.'

She placed a gentle hand on her father's arm.

'That's exactly why I didn't ask! You'd never have refused, and it's such a heavy job.'

Garron opened his mouth to object, but subsided.

'I never thought to see this much of a carry-on at the old Chough,' he muttered at last. 'I hope you've got a couple of hundred saved that you haven't told me about.'

He paused in the act of stuffing a paper back into its envelope.

'Unless we're relying on Kit?' He watched his daughter's expression closely. 'That's it! By the way you're blushing, I'd say you've already asked him to help.'

'I haven't asked Kit for anything!' Jenny protested.

'Well, perhaps he should offer,'

Garron persisted desperately. 'He's mostly the cause of our losing trade earlier this summer with all that dust and lorries and whatnot . . . '

'Dad, don't exaggerate. The harbourside rebuilding attracted lots of new visitors, so everyone's done well out of it. I see you haven't called any more protest meetings!'

'I bet there's still some around here who'd support me.'

'I'm not so sure you want to put it to the test. Most have accepted Kit's ideas were . . . well, if not ideal, at least far better than we first thought.'

'Not everyone!' Garron said crisply.

'Only a few diehards like you and the Biddicks are still grumbling, Dad!'

Garron shuffled the brown envelopes in his hand and pushed them distastefully into a beige cardboard file.

'There's still that playground by the river not finished yet,' he insisted. 'You can't tell me it's safe to stick wooden posts in the mud, not after what I've read about the dangers of rotting!'

'It's soil, not mud. And wooden posts can be protected.'

'Yes — and what chemicals will they let into the ground? But it seems Kit's got all the official approvals wrapped up, whatever we do. I've tried to have my say over that and nobody took any notice.'

'Kit's been turning himself inside out this week discussing what's best — and he's more than taken account of everyone's views,' Jenny said patiently.

Garron faced his daughter, a frown gathering.

'He's recovered his health, hasn't he? So why does he keep needing you to defend him?'

'He doesn't,' Jenny protested. 'I happen to agree with him.'

Garron put down the file and rested his hands on his daughter's shoulders.

'Helping with this project keeps you away from your own business. Surely you can see that, Jenny?' he said, his voice softer. 'Just when we're at sixes and sevens at the Chough now with

Gary being offered that new job and maybe moving out! 'Tisn't fair on you nor anyone!'

Her father continued to study her face.

'There's something else in all this, isn't there?' Garron said, his hands still in place. 'Something you're not saying . . .'

Jenny wasn't ready to confess her newly tender feelings towards Kit. She needed time: time to consider her family, and Bea, of course; time to talk things over — but not yet.

She pushed aside her fringe distractedly.

'I'll tell you, Dad, as soon as I know myself. But for now, the only thing I want is for us to stop arguing!'

A Special Visitor

Gary Hawke took Sophie Gulliver's trembling hand and stepped her down into the boat.

'OK?' he asked. She nodded eagerly, but looked anxious.

'This could be really exciting!' he said encouragingly.

'Are you sure it's a dolphin?'

'So Pauley Biddick told me,' Gary answered. 'I haven't seen it myself, but he reckoned there's a chance in the evenings.'

Will Gulliver followed his wife, and the boat rocked wildly as it took his weight. Gary balanced himself against the side while Sophie grabbed the seat.

'I suppose we'll have to be as still as we can?' she said.

'Yes,' Gary said, checking the engine and shooting a significant glance in Will's direction.

'I can take a hint.' Will grinned. He lowered his solid form with utmost care beside his wife. 'I promise I won't so much as cough.'

'You'd better not!' Sophie said, drawing a steadying breath as Gary eased *Penarren Girl* out of the harbour and into the cove. 'I was all for this adventure when Gary asked us this afternoon, Will, though now we're actually afloat, I'm wondering why I ever agreed to it . . . '

She gave a troubled laugh, and Will linked his arm with hers.

'All under control, Soph. Honestly. It's just a pity we didn't bring the baby . . . '

Sophie's beautiful grey eyes widened in horror.

'Oh, no! I've enough problems getting water-borne as it is. I didn't want Alanna picking that up. She's far better staying with Lily.'

Will squeezed his wife's hand affectionately.

'We'll make a sailor of you yet, love,

won't we, Gary?'

'Relax!' Gary smiled. He steered the little craft expertly over the water. 'I'm glad you've come this far, Sophie. Apologies in advance if we don't actually meet up with Flipper, but I'm afraid these things can't be guaranteed.'

Gary edged the boat into open water. The air was calm. A few craft bobbed near the shore. The water rippled gently and the sound of the waves on the sand came to them like a whisper. In the shelter of the northerly headland he cut the engine.

'When did Paul see the dolphin?' Will asked in a low voice.

'Yesterday, just about here. A youngster came up right beside the inflatable. He said it looked as if it wanted human company.'

'How lovely!' Sophie gazed out to sea. 'Do they often appear on their own?'

Gary shook his head.

'They usually live in groups.'

'So why's this one shown up?' Will asked.

'Well, occasionally, a young male turns up alone,' Gary explained. 'No-one knows the whole reason, but it seems they might get chucked out of the pod for a while. They pal up with humans instead.'

The sky, for once, was as calm as the sea. Sophie's gaze followed the movement of light sparkling on the water.

'Glad you came?' Will asked her.

She smiled briefly.

'This is the real Penarren, my friends!' Gary said quietly.

'Even if we don't see the dolphin, I prefer this to noisy festivals,' Sophie said.

'Didn't you enjoy it at all, Soph?' Will sounded dejected.

'Some of it was fun . . . ' Sophie said without enthusiasm.

'You put a lot of effort into the organisation,' Gary pointed out.

Sophie shrugged.

'Only because Melissa wouldn't take no for an answer.'

'But didn't it make you feel just a bit

more at home?' Will persisted. 'Tell me I did the right thing, Soph!'

Sophie fell silent and turned away from them both. After a while, she scrubbed one hand across her eyes.

'Don't get all upset, love,' Will said, passing her a hankie.

'Sorry,' she muttered. 'I don't know what's wrong with me sometimes.'

'There's nothing wrong with you,' Gary reassured her. 'I reckon you'll be just fine. Look, there's always something here to watch . . . '

He indicated a flock of gulls, lifting and falling in the air off the steep cliffs below the Chough rock.

'It's as if someone's tugging them like kites!' Sophie dried her eyes.

Gary felt the mood in the boat lighten again.

Awkward Moment

'I had an ulterior motive for offering you this trip,' Gary said, choosing his moment.

Will raised his eyebrows.

'You remember that job? I heard this week . . . ' Gary went on.

'You mean you got it? You'll be moving?' Sophie asked.

Gary nodded. He'd worried for so long about Will's reaction, watching his friend now was like waiting for a thread to snap.

'What does Kerensa think?' Sophie wondered.

Will had pressed his lips together and was avoiding Gary's eyes.

'She's pleased, although it's natural her mind's more on the baby just now,' Gary said.

He glanced again at Will, trying to gauge his friend's feelings.

'It seems ages since you went for the interview,' Sophie continued. 'I suppose it's time for congratulations.'

Gary knew that Sophie was doing her best to cover Will's continuing silence. The friendly mood in their little boat was cooling. It was too painful to let that continue.

'Will?' Gary challenged.

'You have to do what's best for you and Kerensa,' Will said heavily. His eyes remained focused far out to sea.

'The thing is . . . if you haven't got a replacement . . . well, if you didn't mind, I could suggest names,' Gary offered.

'It's OK!' Will held up a hand, as if fending off an unwelcome intruder. 'It's my fault. I should have interviewed long since.'

Gary had known this was not going to be easy.

Lucky

Sophie gasped suddenly, breaking the awkward silence. Gary followed the direction of her pointing finger; there — grey, sleek and unmistakably cigar-shaped beneath the surface — was the dolphin. A ruffling of the surface beside the boat, and all three glimpsed its pale, gleaming underside as it rolled in the streaming water.

Sophie inched away from Will to lean over the boat's edge. She watched the dolphin's every move as it leaped and played, spreading water in wide, white arcs. Then, for a few magical minutes, the young creature grew still and seemed to meet Sophie's gaze.

'I wanted to stroke it . . . ' she murmured when finally it swam away.

'It's better not. Or to feed it,' Gary said gently. 'They're wild creatures. We must respect that.'

'I hope it won't become Penarren's nine-day wonder,' Will said.

'We're not allowing the wrong sort of interest,' Gary said firmly. 'Paul has it organised, and I've been helping. There have been a few tragedies in other places in the past, and we want to avoid anything like that.'

'It's pretty amazing, though, isn't it?' Sophie was still smiling. She looked a different girl from the one who'd clung to Gary's hand getting on to the boat. Her eyes shone. She wrapped her arms around herself tightly, as if holding on to something precious.

'You know what? All at once, I feel so *lucky*!' Sophie exclaimed.

Will hugged his young wife. Suddenly both of them were laughing.

Gary steered the *Penarren Girl* back to harbour. Sophie and Will were still smiling when they reached it. Perhaps Will still had concerns about Gary's leaving, and the effect on his business, but Gary could take comfort that this outing seemed to have given Sophie, at least, a new perspective on her future in Penarren, and that could only benefit Will, too.

* ★ *

As he secured the boat and scrambled up the steps, Gary's mobile phone rang. He fished it from his pocket.

'Hi!'

'It's Granfer. Can you hear me OK, Gary?'

'Yes! What's up?'

'Nothing to worry about. Your mum and Kerensa are reaching the hospital about now . . . '

Gary gave a whoop, switched the phone off, and turned to Will and Sophie.

'Sorry — I must go! The baby's on its way!'

Sophie patted his arm.

'Let us know how everything is as soon as you can, Gary!'

Gary wasn't sure any more how his friend would respond. He was relieved when Will Gulliver grinned broadly and thumped his shoulder.

'Good luck, old son! Hope everything goes well,' Will said warmly. 'And Gary . . . thanks for the boat trip! Real good of you to do that.'

'I was glad to, Will!'

'I'm sure we can work things out at the shop. Now — get going, young man. Kerensa will be needing your support!'

Gary sprinted the width of the square and reached the Chough in record time.

Congratulations

Jenny only just heard the bell ring above the din inside the café. She opened the outer door with Ben cuddled on one hip. Paul and Sally stood together on the steps, wreathed in smiles.

'Congratulations!' they said almost in unison.

'Thank you!' Jenny said happily. 'A girl. She arrived very early this morning! Both well. Gary's still with them.'

'What did they decide to call her in the end?' Sally asked, stepping into the hall and kissing first Ben and then Jenny on the cheek.

'Ellen Joy. At least, I think that's right. They didn't make up their minds until the last minute.'

'I saw her and she's Ellie!' Ben said emphatically.

'Well done, Ben!' Paul said, ruffling the boy's hair. 'What do you think of

284

your new sister, then?'

Ben, suddenly overcome by the noise and the attention, hid his face in Jenny's shoulder. Paul laughed and hugged them both in his old, easy way. The three were still together when the doorbell sounded again. Sally answered. It was Kit.

Jenny, smiling, stepped away from Paul and allowed Ben to slip to the floor. Sally took the little boy's hand and led him, skipping with excitement, into the café.

'I wanted to offer my congratulations. And a small gift . . . ' Kit said, a little awkwardly.

'Come in,' Jenny invited him.

'Thanks, but I think it's really a family occasion, isn't it?'

Jenny reached for his hand.

'My dad's declared a party.'

'Congratulations to everyone, then, including Grandma!' Kit said with a smile, stepping inside. He followed his polite kiss on her cheek with a warm, enveloping hug.

'Sorry I haven't seen you for a day or two,' he murmured.

'I doubt if you'd have found me in, we've been so busy!' Jenny said.

Kit's arms stayed round her. Her hands remained, without embarrassment, on his shoulders.

'I've missed you,' she said.

'I've missed you, too,' Kit said, his smile widening.

The cheerfully impatient look on Paul's face was giving way to a frown, which deepened the longer Kit's arms encircled her.

Jenny disentangled herself. She didn't feel like answering questions yet.

'You two had better get to the food before it's all gone,' she said briskly. 'I must go and help Dad.'

Paul moved ahead of Kit into the café, and Jenny hurried towards the kitchen.

Celebrations

The dining room at the Chough was warm, noisy and smelled of Lily Pinch's spiced tea-cake. Over the heads of well-wishers Baz Trudgian had strung balloons and a flowered banner declaring *It's A Girl!* in pink letters.

Paul's parents, Morwenna and Bob, waved to their son from their favourite corner near the window. Sally slipped out of her seat beside them and approached Kit.

'Thought I should warn you,' she murmured, well out of the Biddicks' hearing. 'Morwenna's holding forth about riverside developments. It might be better if you stayed here, and didn't get drawn into an argument.'

'I'll keep my distance.' Kit smiled gratefully. 'Not the proper time for disagreements, is it?'

'Nothing wrong with open discussion,'

Paul interrupted. 'Reckon my mum can say what she likes!'

'Of course . . . I didn't mean . . . ' Kit started. He glanced uneasily at Sally.

'Kit was only reminding us we're here to wet the baby's head,' Sally put in. 'Seems to me we could do without a discussion about bricks and ballast for once!'

'You don't have to stick up for him, Sal. Dear knows, Jenny does that job well enough!' Paul grumbled.

'I didn't know I needed a champion,' Kit said in surprise. 'People seem quite enthusiastic now the harbour development's completed.'

'I'd say that's because they haven't realised there's more goings-on planned beside the river,' Paul said.

'It's hardly a secret.'

Paul squared up to Kit.

'No — but you've made sure it's only getting underway now young Gary's leaving. He's the one who'd have put up the best arguments! He's the one who knows what damage you're like to

288

cause along of the river!'

'Gary . . . leaving?' Kit was nonplussed.

'Don't pretend Jenny hasn't told you!'

'Paul, I don't have to pretend, because she's said nothing!'

'I thought you were business partners,' Paul said. 'More than that, too, from what I've seen for myself this evening!'

Kit stared. He had an inkling of the reason for Paul's irritable mood.

'Jenny's free to choose her friends.'

Kit knew his voice sounded stiff, but he couldn't help it. Paul had been Jenny's friend for a long time, far longer than he had. He felt his mouth go dry.

'A pity you stayed away so long,' Paul growled. 'If you'd been around you'd have known so much more about what makes Penarreners tick!'

Sally pressed a warning hand on Paul's arm.

'He doesn't mean it, Kit,' she said.

'Don't tell me what I mean!' Paul snapped.

Sally glared at him.

'Look . . . ' Kit took a deep breath. 'I'm not going to argue, least of all with a friend. But if you want a meeting, Paul, you only have to ask.'

'It's the asking that sticks in my throat.' Paul's voice was getting louder. 'As if we were *emmets*, and you the squire! I don't like other people taking me for granted, crewmate or not, and that's a fact!'

Sally gave a despairing sigh and went to find Jenny. She found her talking with Lily.

'Do you mean they're disagreeing, Sal?' Jenny laughed. 'That's all they ever do!'

'I think it's serious, this time,' Sally said, drawing Jenny aside.

'You know, I think it's you they're really arguing about,' she said.

Jenny clattered her cup to the saucer.

'Men! I'll give them both a piece of my mind if they ruin this party. Come with me, Sal! Please . . . '

You'd Better Go

By the time Jenny reached the far corner of the room, Paul was very red in the face.

Kit, by contrast, had stuffed his hands in his pockets, and looked pale. Jenny knew them both well enough to guess Kit had reached the point where he'd refused to argue, and this had infuriated Paul far more than if they'd come to blows.

'Paul, you can have a guided tour of the children's study centre any time you like,' Kit said wearily.

Paul glowered.

'You can keep your tours, and your talks — and anything else you think might change me to your way of thinking!' he snarled, one forefinger stabbing out each point on the table. 'I wish you'd never come back!'

'Pauley . . . Kit . . . everyone's here to

celebrate the new baby, not have a set-to,' Jenny said, smiling resolutely. 'I can't have this in my café. After all, I'm a respectable grandmother twice-over now!'

Jenny felt her attempt to lighten the mood fall flatter than a squashed pasty.

Paul thumped his glass on to a nearby table in frustration. It broke.

'That's it!' Jenny had had enough. 'You'd better go . . . '

'Don't worry, I don't feel like staying!' Paul growled. 'I'll just say what I came to say — my very best wishes to Gary and Kerensa.' He took one step and jabbed a finger towards Kit.

'Remember, I'm as good a man at arranging meetings as you are! And there's still plenty who agree with me!'

A curved shard of glass rocked gently on the table as Paul stomped out.

Picking Up The Pieces

Sally, hands on hips, watched him leave.

'I suppose I'd better go after him — see if I can't calm things down a bit,' she said with an apologetic glance at Jenny.

'You're as used to picking up the pieces as I am, Sal!' Jenny replied. 'Go on, I'll clear this . . . '

'I'm certain he didn't intend to break anything, Jenny,' Kit murmured as Sally left.

'I think you'd better go, too,' Jenny said, studiously avoiding his gaze. People nearby were staring. She didn't want to raise suspicions by asking only Paul to leave.

Kit paused, then frowned and placed the gift for baby Ellen on the table between them.

'Then give my best wishes to your

son and his wife,' he said in a tight voice. He moved to touch Jenny's hand, but at the last moment seemed to change his mind. Instead, he picked up his jacket and left.

Watching Kit's retreating back, Jenny thought of their postponed date. It seemed more unlikely to take place than ever. She hurried away to the broom cupboard, her heart pounding. She couldn't tell if she felt angry or just plain miserable. Eventually, she found the dustpan and stared at it for fully a minute before she could remember why it was needed.

★　★　★

'How's your dad?' Daveth asked, lounging on the grassy cliff-top and peering towards the cove on his right.

Bea settled beside him in their favourite meeting place, and gazed towards the shimmering horizon. She loved it that the days were still so warm here, even though it was September.

'He was a real growly old bear yesterday morning, for some reason,' Bea said. 'But apart from that, yes, he's better.'

Daveth flopped flat on the grass.

'Good,' he murmured. He shaded his face with one arm. 'I could do with a kip.'

'Lazy thing!'

Daveth opened one eye.

'Some of us have been working since 6 a.m.,' he protested.

Bea searched for a stem of grass and pulled it.

'Shame!' she said. She trailed the feathered end across Daveth's forehead. 'Don't let me keep you awake.'

'But you do — I can't help it!'

'Well, you shouldn't,' Bea said, giggling.

Serious

Mercurial as ever, her mood changed and she became suddenly serious.

'Daveth, I want to tell you something . . . I've sorted what was bothering me.'

'And what conclusion did you come to?' Daveth asked. He brushed away the tickling end of the grass and sat up.

Bea met his gaze steadily.

'Mum's OK. Dad's better. So now — I'm going to please myself, for a change!'

'And what does Miss Beatrice Venning want?' he asked.

'To stay in Penarren, of course!'

'Don't think to do that on my account, Bea,' Daveth said anxiously.

'But I thought you'd be pleased!' Bea said. She threw away the grassy stem.

'Well, yes, in a way. But you need to think further ahead . . . '

'You sound like my dad,' Bea. grumbled.

'Sorry,' Daveth said. He turned Bea's face towards his and kissed her cheek. 'But have you ever thought your dad might be talking sense?'

'My dad has hardly made any sense lately,' Bea said with a world-weary sigh. 'I thought he'd mellowed a bit, but since this accident he's been in a real state.'

Bea lowered her head, and her voice sank to an anguished whisper.

'Worried about whether he'll be in the lifeboat crew and I don't know what else besides . . . '

Daveth took her hand and pulled her towards him.

'I'm sure it'll be OK.'

Bea didn't look up.

'You don't know what it's like,' she said.

Daveth held her shoulder firmly.

'Don't go pitying yourself, that won't help at all. I used to be like that with my sister. Sally was always way ahead of me — wherever I went, people would ask if I was really Sally Rosewarne's brother, because I couldn't do the stuff she could — beat everyone at running, win the high jump, fly a glider . . . all that.'

'I like Sally,' Bea said. 'Everyone does!'

'So do I, now!' Daveth said with a grin. 'But it wasn't easy growing up as the golden girl's baby brother, I can tell you, and I made it worse by being so cross about it all the time.'

'Does that mean you think I need to grow up?' Bea asked.

Daveth looked away.

'I think you need to spend time thinking about stuff, that's all.'

Beatrice sat back on her heels and flipped a long strand of hair behind one ear.

'I have,' she said.

'What do you mean?'

'I've applied for a proper job.'

'Where?'

'Inland a bit.'

'Newquay?'

'No. A sort-of pub between here and Mawgan.'

'Doing what?'

'Lots of things . . . ' Bea said.

'That sounds a bit vague to me,' Daveth said doubtfully.

'I said I wanted to stay here for always, Daveth, and now I've done something positive about it. That's all! I hoped you'd support me.'

Our Secret

Bea jumped to her feet. Apart from the gentle swish of sound near the rocks, all the way to the horizon the sea shone like glass. She remembered Sophie telling her about seeing the dolphin in the shelter of the headland opposite.

'I wish I could see the dolphin, too,' she whispered, half to herself.

'You know,' Daveth murmured, placing his hands on her shoulders, 'I never expected to become involved with someone like you. And now it's happened, it's great. But I'm worried, Bea, our lives have been so different till now. How can we be sure we'll still get on months, maybe years from now?'

'You mean I'm a spoiled brat?' Bea asked, narrowing her gaze to look far out to sea.

'If I thought that, I wouldn't still be

300

around!' Daveth said. 'But it's happened too quickly. I can't promise how I'll feel in the future, Bea. Not yet. Honestly, I can't.'

Bea turned to face him.

'You must promise something,' she said seriously. 'Don't breathe a word about that job.'

'Always supposing you get it,' Daveth said hesitantly.

'I usually get what I want! But it's our secret, Daveth, OK?'

Daveth frowned.

'I don't like the secrecy bit,' he said.

'Promise!' Bea implored, shaking his arm fiercely. 'I want to surprise my dad — I want to show him I can make grown-up decisions for myself!'

'On one condition.' Daveth paused thoughtfully. 'You must tell me where, and let me give the place the once-over, just for my peace of mind. Deal?'

'Deal!' Bea said with a smile.

She found herself drawn once more into Daveth's embrace. They swayed together, relieved and happy. Bea giggled and rested her head on his shoulder.

At length, Daveth held her away.

'I'll be late for work if I don't go now,' he said. 'Will you be OK getting back?'

'Sure, it's not far. Meet me at the Chough tomorrow after work,' Bea answered.

Daveth gave a nod, and walked briskly along the path towards the next bay and the caravan site where he worked.

Alone Again

Beatrice stood and waved for as long as Daveth remained in her sight. She turned to walk back to Penarren, stopping as she passed the chough rock. From here, she could gaze down to the cove and the tiny buildings that littered the hillside.

The sun was gathering an afternoon veil of mist. Bea fancied to take the smaller path between the ancient rock and the cliff edge, so she could keep in view the headland where lucky Sophie had seen the dolphin. Perhaps, Bea thought, she could persuade Daveth to take her out there some time.

She felt for the hard edge of the granite with one hand. Below the path and the great rock, the grass sloped steeply. Bea watched the sea as it crawled towards the scattered rocks, too far below for her to hear anything but the mildest roar. Even now, she thought dreamily, the dolphin might be there.

She'd lifted her hand from the rock to hold back her wind-blown hair when she felt the path edge crumble gently beneath her feet.

At first, she was unworried. All she needed to do was regain her balance. Her fingers flew to the hand-hold. Her shout as she realised she'd already slipped too far to reach it was lost in a rush of air and the general cry of the gulls.

Only the steep slope lay between her and the cliff edge.

Stifling a monstrous panic, Bea dug her fingers into the sparse earth and pressed herself full-length against it. She didn't dare move her head to look, but she knew without a doubt how abruptly the slope ended somewhere below her sandalled feet. Her legs shook, her fingers ached, but she knew she had to hold on.

Miraculously, a stone was kicked overhead. It leaped from the path and rattled down the slope. Bea sucked a deep breath and shouted. On the path, she heard footsteps stop, hesitate . . . then continue on their way.

A Rude Awakening

'Where is this café you're supposed to be working at, anyway?' Kit Venning asked his daughter over breakfast.

'Round in Veer Bay,' Bea said.

'I know Veer Bay well,' Kit said, frowning. 'I've never heard of the Beachstop!'

'That doesn't mean it's no good,' Bea said defensively.

'Then why have you kept this job a secret until the very morning you're supposed to start work, Bea?'

'I thought you'd be pleased I'd done something for myself. I thought it would be a nice surprise,' she muttered.

'It's a surprise all right,' her father said grimly. 'Almost as upsetting as when I discovered I'd nearly lost my only daughter over Penarren cliff. What has got into you lately, Bea?'

'Nothing!' Bea said, putting up her

hands to brush at the hot tears welling in her eyes. 'You know how much I want to stay here with my friends . . . and Daveth!'

She saw her father's face soften as she fumbled for her handkerchief. He found and offered tissues, but Beatrice turned away.

'All right,' Kit said, putting down the box with a heavy sigh. 'If that's how you want it, my girl, I'll do my best not to interfere. But don't expect me to stand by without speaking my mind!'

'I won't,' Bea said with a sniff.

'It's not like you to be underhand, Bea,' Kit said more quietly. 'I'd prefer it if you didn't keep secrets like this in future.'

He was still frowning when she left the house.

* * *

In the Beachstop's tiny kitchen, Bea's fingers made another dull trail through the greasy, lukewarm water. She reached for the next plate.

Reliving that conversation with her father, misery overwhelmed her. She couldn't understand why he'd found her surprise so unpleasant. She'd meant it to be quite the opposite.

Bea dried the plates with a threadbare towel and stacked them. The Beachstop didn't have many customers, so she was surprised to hear someone at the doorway.

'Anybody home?' Alan Trudgian's voice called.

'Hi!' Bea was glad to welcome a friendly face from Penarren.

'Daveth told me I'd find you here,' he said. 'Thought I'd call in as I was passing and see how you were after your scramble up the cliff . . . '

'I lost my best sandal . . . ' Bea murmured.

Alan gave an easy shrug.

'Not the worst thing that might have happened, all things considered,' he said, smiling.

Bea pulled a face.

'It was awful when I realised! I haven't brought that many decent shoes from Mum's . . . '

Alan leaned on the wobbly counter.

'I hope you're not scaring yourself over that tumble,' he said. 'You did well, you know!'

'What do you mean?' Bea asked. She gazed at Alan's wide, cheerful features.

'True, you got yourself into trouble,' he said. 'But you got yourself out of it again, didn't you?'

Bea stared.

'I don't know what I'd have done if you hadn't come along,' she whispered.

'You'd already climbed back up to the path by the time I got there,' Alan said stoutly. 'Never saw a braver scramble!'

Bea looked at him disbelievingly.

'All I can remember is hearing footsteps going away. I didn't think anyone would come back. That's when I knew I had to do something. I've never yelled so loudly in my life!'

'I thought I heard a faint cry.' Alan

grinned. 'That's why I ran back. But make no mistake, you were the only one that got yourself up, scratched knees and all.'

'I was very glad to see you,' Bea said.

'All I did was help you along the path,' the youngest Trudgian insisted. He pushed himself upright and made for the door. 'You didn't let the panic get the better of you, Bea! Remember that!'

He waved and was gone. Bea dropped the tea towel over the sink and rushed after him.

'Thank you for everything, Alan!' she called. 'And thanks for coming to see how I am!'

'All part of the service!' he called back, saluting.

Action Stations

Thoughtfully, Bea watched Alan go then returned to empty her washing-up bowl. Water glugged down the inadequate plughole.

She sighed and glanced around inside the little hut's kitchen, wondering what Jenny would say about the state of it. It bore no resemblance to the one at the Chough.

Bea was scrubbing the back of the sink so hard when the kiosk's owner came in that she didn't hear him.

'I want you to make cheese sandwiches, special,' he said.

He dumped a creaking basket on the counter. Bea turned, wringing out her cloth.

'I need to wash my hands first,' she said.

The café owner smiled complacently, nodded towards the greasy sink and hurried out.

'But the water's cold,' Bea called after him urgently. 'There ought to be soap and a nailbrush . . . and where do you keep the clean towels?'

She was questioning the empty air. She hurled herself at the door only to see her employer's van disappearing along the beach road back to Penarren.

Someone had to take responsibility if the wretched man wouldn't, Bea decided, taking a very deep breath.

Before she made so much as one cheese sandwich, she'd heat some water, find what cleaning materials lurked beneath the sink, and make sure all those surfaces were scrubbed clean if it took her the rest of the morning.

By the start of her third day, Bea thought her workplace looked a little less shabby. She'd found an elderly, unopened tin of scouring powder hidden deep in a cupboard and put it to good use. Other things — fresh cloths, disinfectant and a scrubbing brush — she'd brought with her from home. Even so, she was beginning to realise that all her efforts couldn't transform a kitchen that had never been properly looked after. She'd never known anywhere with so many hard-to-clean corners.

Later that afternoon, as she was making a pot of tea and thinking of Daveth, he appeared at the serving hatch.

'You startled me!'

'How are you, Bea? I've been that worried since I saw you last, all covered in scratches.'

They'd met only once since the cliff-top incident, when Bea hadn't been looking or feeling her best.

'Alan Trudgian came over earlier this week. You might have visited before now!' Bea said reproachfully, refilling the teapot.

'We've got a lot of end of season repairs on at the moment, Bea. I did tell you. Anyway, Alan told me you were doing OK.'

'Fancy a cup of tea?' Bea asked, slightly mollified.

'I'll come inside.' Daveth stepped through the doorway. 'I promised to check this place out, and I haven't done it yet.'

Bea thrust a mug of tea into his hand. 'No need,' she said. 'I'm in charge now.'

'Not the smartest place, I'd say . . . ' Daveth continued moving around the hut, taking care to peer into the corners.

'You should have seen this dump three days ago,' Bea said. 'My hands are scrubbed sore!'

'You've done all right. But did you notice that the fridge isn't working? This cheese will be growing its own fur coat come the end of the week.'

Bea sighed. She'd done her best, but with a sinking heart realised that this time she needed back-up. She tightened her apron strings.

'OK, I admit you were right to warn me,' she said, suddenly impatient.

She saw Daveth glance at her and smile.

'That's my girl,' he said.

'Since you know all about this stuff, Daveth Rosewarne,' Beatrice said briskly, 'you can tell me how and where I report these conditions as quickly as possible!'

Piglet

'I can hardly believe it!' Kit said, smiling. He subsided on to the wind-toughened bench overlooking the cove. 'We have each other's company for a whole evening.'

He patted the seat. Jenny had offered to cook supper, but they'd decided to take a walk first. She moved away from the cliff's edge and sat close to lean her head on Kit's shoulder.

'What were you looking at?' Kit asked.

'Over to Veer Bay. Do you know what 'veer' means?'

'I don't think anyone ever told me . . . or if they did, I must have forgotten.'

'Piglet,' Jenny enlightened him.

Kit chuckled.

'So my daughter's working in Piglet Bay, is she?' He sighed and pulled a face. 'But perhaps she wouldn't see the funny side at the moment.'

'She's not exactly been in clover, I gather,' Jenny said. 'I heard she got Environmental Health to visit her workplace, though. Good for her.'

'My daughter hasn't been taking me into her confidence lately,' Kit said. 'I find it hard to appreciate her stubborn refusal to quit the wretched job. On the plus side, though, she's certainly showing responsibility. She gets more like her mother every day.'

'Or her father!' Jenny grinned.

Kit smiled and stretched his legs with the luxurious attitude of a man who has earned time off and is determined to make the most of it.

Enchanted Evening

Far below them the tide was out, leaving a wide, golden margin of sand that gleamed in the evening light. Darkness arrived swiftly at this time of year, but while the orange sun still glowed above the horizon the evening seemed to stretch ahead of them for ever.

'How's the leg?' Jenny asked.

'Good!' Kit said. 'I'm back on the *Etta*! I was a bit worried after our recent falling-out that Paul might not want me there, but he was OK. I don't want ill-feeling on board the *Etta*, and neither does he. It's been a good feeling to get back — like rejoining my family.'

'Just when mine is planning to leave,' Jenny reflected. 'Gary and I . . . I know we don't always agree, either, but I'm going to miss him and the family. If only I could be sure that the poor things could find a decent place to rent near his new job . . . '

Gulls launched themselves off the cliff and drifted on the air, uttering an occasional cry.

'Come on!' Kit said, suddenly restless. 'Let's walk. Down on the beach. We can roll up our trousers and paddle . . . '

Jenny stood, making great show of the light, floating summer skirt she was wearing that evening in honour of their date.

'And what if one of us is wearing something that the other hasn't noticed yet?' she asked.

'I'm noticing now!' Kit said quickly. 'You look lovely.'

They laughed and held hands, matching strides as they walked.

Deeper Waters

'About Gary . . . ' Kit began as they approached the beach. 'Venning's has flats to let — they're similar to those renovations near Penarren harbour. If he — or more importantly, perhaps, Kerensa — liked the idea . . . '

Jenny stopped.

'Where?' she asked.

'Polcreek Mill,' he said, renewing his hold on her hand. 'So long as it's near enough to Gary's workplace . . . '

'Kit, that would be great!'

'It's not too far from Penarren, either. If they say yes, I'll consider it a deal.'

Jenny hugged Kit's arm gratefully.

'These days youngsters must imagine they'll be at home with their parents for ever,' she said with feeling. 'And the situation's trickier here than almost anywhere. I'm sure they'll jump at it.'

'I hoped you wouldn't mind . . . ' Kit said.

'Mind?'

'You weren't keen for me to offer help with the Chough.'

'That was different,' Jenny replied shortly.

'But surely everything's changed now?' Kit persisted.

By this time, they were moving steadily through the shallow waves. Delicate edges of foam curled at their ankles. Kit halted and drew Jenny close.

'Hasn't it?' he asked again.

Jenny hugged him, both arms around his waist.

'You know it has,' she whispered. 'But that doesn't mean you have to rush into any commitments at the Chough that you might not want to keep to later.'

She was dismayed to feel Kit break away.

'I suppose a failed relationship in my past isn't exactly a recommendation for staying power,' he said sadly. 'Is that really how you feel?'

'No!' Jenny cried.

'What, then?'

'I agree we need to talk about the Chough — some time. But, to my mind, that's separate from us — from our feelings for each other!'

'The Vennings have never been a good bet as far as Penarren's concerned,' Kit continued, almost as if he hadn't heard her. 'It doesn't seem to matter what we do!'

He kicked his way fretfully into deeper water. Jenny felt her eyes sting in a way that had nothing to do with the salt breeze.

'Don't say that, Kit!'

'What would convince you to allow me alongside, then?'

'For once, the Chough is beside the point! You're the one that's important to me.'

She reached him just as a higher wave engulfed their knees.

'I should have remembered: every seventh wave is bigger,' Kit murmured, looking down. 'Sorry — is your hem wet?'

Jenny wrung out the dripping edge of her skirt.

'I don't care if it is,' she said. 'I need to talk sense into you, Kit Venning, so we'll just keep walking until I have.'

They'd reached the far side of the cove. The rim of the sun had dissolved along the horizon.

'I'm listening,' Kit said, lifting her hand to his cheek as they turned to walk up the beach.

Changes

Here and there among the small, grey houses, sharp points of light glowed. A few fishing boats were drawn up on the beach, their ropes rattling the masts, their shapes darkening in the twilight.

'I think we need to get away from only thinking about work,' she said.

'That's what I thought I was doing when I came back to Penarren,' Kit said. 'Everything was going to be simpler, somehow once I got home.'

'And it wasn't?'

'I'm annoyed I didn't see the obvious pitfalls!'

'You're not clairvoyant,' Jenny said. 'And if it's any consolation, I'm not either! I never thought this would happen . . . '

She swallowed.

'When I lost Dan,' she said after a while, 'I thought of moving away, of taking my son and myself somewhere where the cliffs didn't loom and the sea didn't roar at night.'

Kit gently squeezed her hand as they walked.

'But you stayed . . . ' he said.

'Because I realised this was home and pulling up my roots would have been impossible on top of the grief.'

'So you made a go of Dan's business instead?'

'Then you arrived . . . '

'Making changes you didn't want?'

Jenny smiled.

'That's my point. After so much time cherishing what Dan had left me, the last thing I expected was to welcome your new ideas. But after those endless arguments and discussions, well . . . I could see they made sense.'

No Doubts

The marram whispered around their feet as they reached the dunes. They came to a halt beneath the sign of the Chough café.

'By the time you'd convinced me, something else had happened. I warned you once about the Penarren Effect. Do you remember?'

'That nothing turns out as you expect?'

'I thought I could never care for anyone as I cared for Dan Hawke,' Jenny said. 'But that time you were hurt and lying in the hospital, I felt I'd hit the water, too. I couldn't doubt my feelings for you after that, much less deny them.'

Kit held her close.

'You know that's how I feel, too. No doubts, not this time.'

The Chough sign moved in the

breeze. Jenny glanced up at the still-bright eye and the red, faded leg of the ancient Cornish emblem.

'You faced changes just by coming home, Kit,' she said quietly. 'Now we're both contemplating so many more. I reckon we need to get to know each other — but not the same way we did while we were battling with building schedules and workmen . . . '

They kissed before going inside, the Chough groaning loudly over their heads.

'I apologise for the less-than-musical serenade,' Jenny murmured.

Kit grinned wickedly.

'I promise I won't offer to mend it!' he said. 'At least . . . not until I'm asked.'

Down By The Riverside

Garron had promised to meet Lily and Ben outside Gulliver's the following day. It took him longer than usual to reach the shop, pushing through the lunchtime crowds at the harbourside.

Will greeted him as he reached the doorway.

'Your window display's looking handsome, Mr Gulliver!' Garron remarked.

'All my Sophie's work, too,' Will said proudly.

Garron gazed at the rippling, soft lengths of cloth scattered with beautiful sea-coloured pendants and brooches, which glittered where they caught the sun.

'Kerensa's been wearing one like that . . . ' Garron pointed at a pendant in a dolphin design.

'Sophie made a few of those,' Will murmured.

'Reckon she's feeling more settled now, do you?' Garron asked seriously.

'I believe she is,' Will said, easing the back of his neck with his hand and smiling broadly.

A group of tourists trundled past. Some peeled off from the group, and smiling, sauntered into Will's shop.

'Plenty visitors still about, for the time of year,' Garron observed.

'They're heading for those art and craft outlets beside the harbour that Kit Venning restored. Made quite a difference to us, I can tell you,' Will said.

'Not pulling custom away, then?'

Will shook his head.

'Not at all, Cox'n. I'd say quite the opposite!'

Garron felt pleased for Will. This solid young man had taken a gamble coming here with his family, and he and Sophie had worked hard for success. Garron was relieved to hear that Sophie seemed happier these days, too.

*   *   *

He looked up to see Lily Pinch weaving her way through the throng. In one hand she carried a straw bag and in the other she clasped Ben's wrist. As they drew closer, the little boy wriggled free and pelted headlong towards his great-grandfather. Garron caught him.

'There you are, my babby!' He beamed, lifting the boy a little off the pavement.

Ben launched into a detailed description of precisely where he hoped they'd have their picnic that afternoon. Garron set the boy back on his feet and listened.

'Are we off down the stream, then?' Garron appealed to Lily when she stopped beside him.

'That's right,' she said, slightly breathless. 'It's a fair walk, my dear. Hope you don't mind.'

Garron captured his great-grandson's hand and held it firmly.

'I reckon it's our mission to tire the lad out if we can, Lily! He'll sleep all the better. Good of you to look after him while Kerensa's tending to his sister. Where to first?'

'That playground place ... ' Lily said.

'No!' Ben said urgently, bouncing on his toes. 'It's not a playground, Nana says. It's a little park for *being* in.'

Garron pressed his lips together. He hadn't yet visited Kit's final project at the new riverside development, and he wasn't sure he wanted to. But if Lily had planned it, and Ben had set his heart on it ...

'Come on, then!' Lily said with a smile. She took Ben's other hand and they made their way across the square. They skirted the Chough car park, and crunched across increasingly rough ground until they reached the riverside path. A further walk, and a low wooden fence came into view.

'There it is!' Ben squealed. 'Can we go inside? Can we eat our sandwiches now?'

'Have patience, young Ben!' Lily said. She turned to Garron.

'Well, there 'tis, Garron Trelawney! What do you make of it?'

The fence was lower than he'd imagined. It blended in well enough.

'I'm not sure, Lily, and that's the truth.'

'Perhaps we should go and see.'

'I never knew it was open.'

'It's not official till next week, I believe,' Lily said. 'But Kit said most things are up and running . . . '

Gentle Soul

Still holding Ben, Garron pushed the gate into a wide enclosure. He barely recognised the area as the one where he'd played as a child, and yet when he looked more closely, not as much had changed as he'd feared. There were still thistles and mallow and rough grasses growing along one edge, while a long, slatted wooden path twisted ahead through an area full of dramatically spiked leaves.

Safely inside, Ben danced away, eager to see what lay past the next corner. There was a howl of delight, and Garron and Lily rounded the bend to find him clambering over a seat carved into a rock. Bushes nearby hid a gentle slope, which in turn led to half-a-dozen stout wooden tables and a picnic area where other families were already sitting.

Lily unpacked the sandwiches.

'"Tis quite busy,' she observed.

'Yes,' Garron agreed. He didn't feel inclined to comment further until he'd had a good look around.

'Ben likes it,' Lily pointed out.

Garron watched the energetic little boy who reminded them all so much of Dan Hawke.

'Just like you, I worried how this place would turn out,' Lily said, finally plumping herself down beside Garron. She passed him a sandwich.

'When Kit was a boy and I helped take care of him, I remember how hard he tried to do whatever his dad wanted of him,' Lily continued.

Garron frowned, not yet understanding.

'Well, he became a successful enough businessman, I suppose,' he said thoughtfully.

'But now he's been back home a while, and especially since he's got to know your Jenny, I do see more of his mother in him,' Lily went on. 'Mrs

Venning was a gentle soul. Loved her garden and all the plants and birds, she did . . . '

Garron swept one hand wide.

'So you feel all this shows Kit's more sensitive side?' he asked. 'I must admit it's not what I imagined. Look there . . .'

Where the stream flowed alongside the new development, the ducks had taken up residence. Garron thought they'd probably discovered it was a good place to find food, but their presence made the spot live again as it did in his memory.

Ben zoomed near again, and Lily held out a cake. He sat to eat it, and then tugged Garron's hand.

'Let's go over here now!' he said.

Garron brushed his crumbs to the grass and allowed Ben to tow him into a log cabin, screened by low bushes. Inside it was brightly lit and smelled of linseed and new, clean floors. In no time, Garron found himself absorbed in showing his great-grandson how to press different coloured buttons to light up an information map.

Ben turned to him with a brilliant smile.

'Granfer! Press that one and see the bird's nest! This is fun!'

Throughout the afternoon, Garron found himself grudgingly renewing his opinion of Kit's ideas. When Will Gulliver had benefited from increased trade on one side of the cove, and children like his Ben could enjoy the riverside afresh on the other, perhaps it was time for him to think again.

If the Penarren ducks had adapted to the changes, Garron found himself thinking, maybe its former coxswain should, too.

* * *

The large room at the Merrymaid was hot and full of people by the time Sally reached it. It was a good sign — this fund-raising evening for the lifeboats must be going well.

She looked around, coffee in hand. In

any gathering she thought, smiling to herself, Pauley Biddick would be the one person you'd spot immediately. He'd be the one surrounded by friends trading friendly banter. This evening, he was not only at the hub, but also conducting some kind of auction.

'Now — what am I bid for this beautiful tablecloth, embroidered by none other than our lovely Lily of Pinch Cottage?' Paul asked. He caught sight of Sally and winked.

'What do you say, Sal?' he called. 'How do you start the bidding for this delicate, amazing, artistic . . .'

'Five pounds!' Sally interrupted, quickly getting into the spirit of things. Paul had the knack of drawing people together.

'Five pounds I'm bid!' he said. 'Who's going to make it ten?'

'Eight!' someone shouted.

'Nine!' another cried.

Finally, Sally bid again at ten pounds fifty and won.

When all the items had been

auctioned, Paul brought the pretty cloth across to her, bowing as he presented it.

'Thanks, Sal. You came in just when I needed someone to set things off right.'

'All in a good cause,' Sally said, laughing. She looked inside the rustling tissue-paper packet. 'It's pretty, isn't it? I'd never have the patience to sit and sew anything like that.'

'Me, neither,' Paul said seriously.

The thought of Pauley Biddick sitting and sewing a fine seam caused Sally to roll her eyes.

'Are you saying I'd be no good at it?' the deputy coxswain demanded, grinning. 'I'd have you know every man of the sea has to be able to turn his hand to anything!'

'And every woman of the sea, too,' Sally pointed out.

'Of course,' Paul said soberly. 'We couldn't do without you.'

Sympathetic

Sally glanced around and noticed that the tables, which earlier on had been heaped with cakes and biscuits for sale, were now empty. She saw Paul's mum, Morwenna, preparing to wipe them down.

'I should lend a hand . . . ' she began, but Paul caught her arm.

'Before you go, Sal . . . I wanted to say thanks for . . . well, for calming me down that time I fell out with Kit.'

'That's what friends do, Paul, look out for each other.'

'I'm coming round now to how things are changing around Penarren. A few of us have spoken to Kit about a permanent group to keep an eye on this conservation place beside the river and head off any problems before they arise.'

'So you can have your say when you

want it?' Sally said. 'That sounds better than Kit offering lectures and walk-abouts!'

'My mum's idea!' Paul beamed.

'Good for her! Nobody says no to Morwenna!'

'I just wanted you to know how much I appreciated you, Sal.'

'You're welcome.'

'The truth is, I was more upset with Jenny than Kit that evening.'

'Do you want to talk about it?' Sally asked.

Paul nodded.

'I'm OK, but I ought to have realised, I see that now.'

'Realised what?' Sally persisted. Sometimes she wondered why Paul, who could chat so freely in a group, found it so hard to express himself sometimes to her.

'Jenny . . . and me . . . ' He stopped.

Sally rested one hand on his arm.

'I guessed your feelings for Jenny ages ago,' she said.

Relieved, Paul gave a wry smile.

'There's nobody more sympathetic than you, Sal,' he said. He shifted restlessly from one foot to the other.

'I'm still listening.'

'It wasn't Jenny's fault,' Paul went on. 'She told me the truth when she said there wasn't anyone else.'

'And then, at the party, you saw her with Kit, and doubted it?' Sally asked quietly.

'I jumped to conclusions. I thought she'd tried to deceive me.'

'Jenny would never do that to anyone.'

'I know.'

Direct Approach

There was a crash from the kitchen, and a cheerful wave of guffaws reached them from across the room.

'Somebody's dropped a tin pail,' Sally observed.

'Let's hope it's not a full collecting box,' Paul said dryly. 'There'll be a lot to pick up.'

Morwenna waved a cloth in the air, inviting help, but neither of them was ready to break off yet.

Sally turned to Paul, wanting to say more. She wasn't yet sure how much.

'Jenny seems very happy these days,' she said carefully. 'How are things between you now?'

Paul gave a wide smile.

'We're friends. Always will be!'

'Nothing more . . . ?'

Paul shook his head, still smiling. A

further gale of laughter from the kitchen distracted him.

Sally took a deep breath.

'So what about us, then, Paul?'

Annoyingly, her usually strong and vibrant voice came out in a squeak. The pretty silk scarf she'd tied at her neck felt stifling.

'Us?' Paul's attention was still directed towards the kitchen.

'Are we friends, too?'

'Couldn't do without you, Sal!' Paul said happily. He clapped her shoulder. 'You're my best mate!'

Sally remembered how warmly Paul had welcomed her when she'd started on the *Etta*. The way he'd helped her with the training . . . and said how much he appreciated her direct approach.

'What I really mean is . . . ' Sally began, and couldn't finish.

'Not like you to run out of words,' Paul said, smiling. 'Any more'n me!'

Sally closed her eyes for a second, and then dived in.

'But that's just it! Not saying anything! It's become a habit with us, hasn't it?'

She'd held back the words just as long as she could, and now here they were tumbling abroad like foolish clowns.

'But I couldn't! Say anything, I mean. Not until I knew! I wanted to say it so many times, but I was scared! Of upsetting you, or Jenny, . . . or your parents, . . . or even the crew on the *Etta*! Oh, Paul, you must see how impossible it's been!'

'Sally,' Paul said patiently. 'What's been so impossible to say? To me, of all people?'

Sally gazed into Paul's kind but puzzled blue eyes. Despite her frustration with him at that moment, she never wanted him to change. But if she didn't say something now, he was never going to guess . . .

'Pauley Biddick, I love you.'

The world seemed to stand still. Sally was conscious that the Merrymaid was

344

as boisterous as ever, but it was as if she and Paul were standing in their own silent bubble.

Paul was focusing on her the sort of calm, intense look she'd normally only seen when they were heading to a rescue on the *Etta*.

'And I want to know if you feel the same,' Sally added almost in a whisper, doing her shaky best to smile.

She lifted her hand from his. Perhaps he didn't feel as she did, after all. In a room full of people, Sally Rosewarne had never felt so alone.

The next moment, Paul wrapped her tenderly in his arms and banished that feeling for good.

'I've been slow on the ol' uptake, haven't I, my dear soul?' he murmured against her cheek. 'Ignoring how you felt all this time.'

'You weren't to know,' Sally said, breathing out at last, her hands twisting against his pullover to draw him closer.

Morwenna signalled to her son again.

Paul waved to his mother in acknowledgement, but his gaze lingered on Sally's face.

'It's warm in here, Sal,' he said softly, tidying the disarranged scarf at her neck. 'I don't know about you, but I could do with a breath of fresh air. Fancy a walk? Seems to me we have some catching up to do.'

Decisive

Kit Venning sat at a small table in the bustling back courtyard of the Merrymaid, waiting for Bea to join him. The evening sun fell warmly across his back and slowly his shoulders relaxed. It had been a busy day.

His lifeboat pager buzzed. It was about to get busier.

Calling out to Fred Trudgian to ask him to let Bea know where he was when she arrived, Kit set off for the station.

Maroons clapped two sharp warnings in the clear sky as Kit ran. Alan Trudgian's car drew out from the Merrymaid and stopped on the downhill road.

'Jump in!' Alan leaned over and held the door open.

'Thanks! What's up?'

'Some holidaymaker misjudging the

tide, I expect . . . '

They sped around the curve of the harbour, rocking to a halt outside the lifeboat station.

'Coastguard reports a child missing from the cove,' Paul announced. His gaze fell on Kit, with Alan beside him. 'As well as the *Etta*, we'll need the D-class. Close into the headland, maybe below the Chough rock. OK?'

⋆　⋆　⋆

Kit, by now heaving on his suit, gave a quick thumbs up. The inshore boat would go with its crew of Kit, Paul and Alan, sheltered by the *Etta* in deeper water until needed.

The familiar routine of klaxon, lights and slap of ropes launched the *Etta*. The D-class *Decisive* arrived to bob in its slipstream. Thankfully, the sky remained calmer than the sea, but Kit's face stung from salt spray on every side. He felt every lurch of the waves.

'OK?' Paul shouted from the bows of

the *Decisive*. Alan nodded. Kit clapped his wet hand on the helmsman's shoulder.

The tough little craft was designed for shallower waters, but it would need all Paul's experience to keep them trouble-free in the intricate pattern of wave and wash they were entering. The rocks that lay around the base of the far cliff had never looked so intimidating.

'Any news?' Alan shouted. They were still following the *Etta*.

'Small boy . . . white shirt, blue dungarees,' Paul hollered.

Lofted suddenly out of a trough and on to a high, choppy wave, Kit saw nothing but the tumble of half-submerged rocks. With Alan, he gripped the side of the *Decisive* as they fell back. The *Etta* crackled instructions.

'Got him!' Paul cried, turning the boat.

Race Against Time

The tide running in hit the backwash rolling out from beneath the cliffs. Black rocks sharp as tacks punctured the water's surface wherever Kit looked. He clung on again as the *Decisive* bucked, uncertain how close in they might get. But if there was a way, he trusted Paul to find it. Stomach jolted by another swooping lift, Kit caught the gleam of blue and white at the base of the cliffs.

'There!' he yelled in Alan's ear.

They held on as Paul turned the *Decisive*, leaving a curved wake.

'I'll let the tide take her in backwards!' Paul shouted.

Running the engine in bursts meant he had some chance of keeping their bows clear of the rocks, but each time Paul made headway he had to abandon the effort. After every attempt, he was forced to speed the boat to safe, open water before trying again.

'Couldn't a helicopter get a line down?' Kit gasped. They'd found the boy quickly enough, but with the tide rushing in he was afraid they were losing time.

''Copter's fifteen minutes away yet!' Paul shouted, controlling the *Decisive* for another run.

'Don't worry, Kit. We'll get 'un . . . ' Alan muttered.

By now the little crew were drenched. Kit's back, arms and shoulders were aching with tension before Paul manoeuvred the boat close once more. The sun gleamed beneath a cloud, illuminating wave tops and the vulnerable figure on a rocky ledge. Kit's mouth dried as the boy turned a tiny, pale face towards the sound of the approaching engine.

'It's Ben!' he shouted, grabbing the side.

'This'll be our best chance!' Paul yelled at the same moment above a rush of surf.

A swell lifted them. Unsure Paul had judged it right, Kit held back his instinct to act until the last second. But as a backwash boosted the boat he recognised Paul had gained them enough height.

Just before the D-class pancaked again in the shallow waters pelting off the ledge, Kit lunged. He was at full stretch before he swept a white-faced Ben into the boat.

Wet, gasping and exultant, Kit wrapped Jenny's grandson close to his heart.

The engine growled and the *Decisive* sped them all into open water.

'It's OK, now, Ben. OK,' Kit found himself saying, over and over.

He thought how much Ben reminded him of Dan Hawke. He thought of Jenny. Relief flooded through him.

★   ★   ★

A too-silent Ben suddenly regained his voice in the cabin of the *Etta*. He didn't stop talking until he was delivered at last to his anxious family. Then he bawled.

Everyone looked surprised, except Garron, who seemed to be expecting it.

'You'm got a good pair of lungs there, my babby,' he said, his voice rough with emotion as he handed his great-grandson into Kerensa's warm embrace. The former coxswain turned to the D-class crew.

'Thanks, lads!' he said.

He shook their hands in turn. Kit was last in the line, and Jenny's father held his hand longer than the others. Garron said nothing, but finally patted Kit's arm and returned to his family. Kit, unwilling to intrude, stayed where he was. Glad of their reconciliation as he was, he wished Jenny had been with her father. Conversations were always easier when she was around.

Ben stopped sobbing.

Kit took a deep breath and found Paul beside him.

'Well done from me, too,' the deputy coxswain murmured.

'I'll stand you a whopping Chough pasty some time for getting the boy out o' that lot, my ol' lover!' Alan Trudgian said, wiping his hand down his face.

'It was OK, thank goodness!' Kit said, easing his shoulders.

Paul's hand gripped him.

'It might not have been,' he said.

'Was it as close-run as it felt?' Kit asked.

'Closer,' Paul said soberly. 'Good job you were always a tall 'un, Kitto Venning!'

Kit was sharply reminded of the third boy who'd often led their small gang of friends.

'I do reckon Danny Hawke would have said we made a good team this day,' Paul Biddick added, as if reading Kit's thoughts.

'Thanks,' he said, smiling.

★ ★ ★

Gary Hawke was at Gulliver's, helping Will and Sophie to clear the shop of leftover Penarren festival paraphernalia. It was a problem to decide what should go where.

'Are these yours?' Will asked, holding up a formidable pair of scissors. Gary shook his head.

'Dunno, Will. You keep them.'

'They're good ones . . . ' Will said doubtfully.

'In that case, they're most likely yours!' Gary said.

Will shrugged, and stowed them in a box.

'Those marker-pens will be useful for my new job, though,' Gary said, pointing to a brightly coloured packet on the floor.

Will handed them over.

'When are you leaving?' Will asked.

'In a week . . . '

'How are you doing with the packing, up at the Chough?'

'Mum and Kerensa have it under control,' Gary said. 'It's nice to get out from under everyone's feet, if I'm honest, what with all the upset earlier over Ben's adventures.'

'Did you find out what happened?' Sophie cuddled her baby daughter closer.

'Kerensa left the baby with Mum, took Ben to the beach, then must have dozed off. Ellie's been waking us such a lot in the night. Kerensa feels so guilty. Mum said she must never blame herself.'

'We all know what a handful Ben can be,' Sophie said.

Will shuffled a pile of papers into a rubbish sack.

'I suppose Kit's riverside park will be good for local children, as well as tourists,' he said thoughtfully.

'Having a nice, secure area is a help,' Gary agreed.

'Not that we should mollycoddle our kids,' Sophie said unexpectedly.

Gary smiled at her. Sophie's regained confidence had altered her opinion on most things.

'We shan't keep Ben still for long,' Gary said. 'He's so like my dad!'

'From what I hear Dan Hawke was a strong character,' Will said.

'My mum, too,' Gary said. He grinned at a sudden thought. 'I hope no-one mentions our plan to her too soon!'

'What plan?' Will heaved a full sack of shredded paperwork and boxes to join others beside the door.

'Haven't you heard?' Sophie said in a stage whisper. ' 'Cady's Cousins' are back!'

'Musical mates . . . ' Gary explained fondly. 'Almost my family at one time. They're coming to play us out. Granfer reckoned we shouldn't worry Mum about setting up the evening, so I went ahead and sorted it out.'

'Speaking of families,' Will said thoughtfully, 'I've heard it's getting serious — your mum and Kit Venning.'

'I reckon so, too.'

'What do you think of it, then, Gary?'

'I admit I didn't like it much at first. But . . . let's just say I've come to appreciate Kit's good points,' Gary replied.

'He's changed since he came back,' Will observed.

'That goes for us all, I think,' Gary agreed.

'Things can come right when people care for each other,' Sophie murmured dreamily. 'You've only got to see Paul and Sally walking hand in hand to know that . . . '

'There's a full moon this week. Should be romantic enough, even for someone like Kit,' Will said with a wink.

'He might find my mum will do the asking if he doesn't!' Gary grinned.

'Only thing is . . . Bea told me her dad's determined to get her away from that job, and she's not budging until it suits her,' Sophie put in. 'I hope that won't mean more family wrangles for them.'

Misunderstandings

On one of her irregular days off, Bea was making tea in the kitchen at Trenfos, while her father was doing his best to assemble a salad for lunch. He was expecting Jenny to arrive at any moment.

'I told you, Dad!' Bea said. 'I wanted to make sure the changes at the Beachstop were done properly. Not to bail out as soon as I'd called the inspector . . .'

'And I'm saying you should have left that place as soon as you realised it wasn't properly run, sweetheart,' Kit replied.

Bea faced her father, tea caddy in hand.

'Is that what you'd have done?' Bea popped three teabags into the pot. 'Or Jenny?'

'I might have had enough sense not

to take the job in the first place,' Kit muttered.

His knife skidded on the plate and chunks of tomato scattered over the kitchen top.

'You didn't have to take that job,' he persisted.

'But I *did* take it!' Bea said stubbornly. 'Once I started, I couldn't see any . . . any *honourable* way out, except by seeing it all through.'

'There's nothing dishonourable about leaving a job if you've done all you can,' Kit said.

Bea sighed, and clattered cups.

'Look — if it's a matter of losing wages, I can make it up to you,' Kit said.

Bea stared at him. A familiar, unwelcome irritation fell around her like an itchy blanket. Why did every discussion with Dad have to boil down to this?

'Money isn't the only reason I do things!' she snapped.

Kit chopped a cucumber into inelegant slices.

'Try taking on anything without it, my girl!'

'I don't agree, Dad!'

'I don't mean you can't also act out of goodness . . . or . . . or love, all other things being equal, Bea,' Kit said. 'But you still need money to do it.' His voice tightened. 'You always misunderstand me!'

Bea wished her dad wouldn't get worked up and then make out he was oh-so-calm. She couldn't pretend she was.

'You can say what you like!' Her voice rose. 'I had my own ideas. And for once maybe I didn't want to listen to yours!'

'Beatrice!' Kit's face was thunderous.

The doorbell rang. Bea rattled spoons on to saucers and fled to answer it, her eyes stinging.

All Grown Up

Jenny stopped in the hall and looked at Bea curiously. 'Chopping onions?' she enquired.

Bea shook her head, but couldn't trust herself to speak.

In the kitchen, Kit placed a careful kiss on Jenny's cheek.

'How's young Ben?' he asked.

'Cheerfully hindering his mother!' Jenny said, kissing him back. 'I know it's been said, but we're all so grateful to the crew. My dad's full of admiration — it must have been the trickiest shout so far, especially for you.'

Kit nodded, then turned in search of the salad dressing.

'It's so nice to be waited on,' Jenny said serenely.

Bea guessed this change of subject was to spare her dad's blushes. Jenny sank on to a high stool and slid her shoulder bag to the floor.

'Dad and Lily love lunchtimes at the Chough, so fortunately I don't feel guilty about leaving others in charge,' she continued.

'Good to hear your place is keeping busy,' Kit said, putting bread rolls on the table.

'Penarren's done well this year,' Jenny said. 'That hasn't been the case everywhere.'

'Such as Veer Bay,' Bea put in.

'I heard about your tussle with the owners. Good for you, keeping on top of the problem. How are things now?'

'Improving, thanks,' Bea replied. 'Daveth's helped.'

'With cleaning materials supplied from this kitchen,' Kit said sharply. 'I hope that won't continue!'

'It won't now I've left, will it?' his daughter demanded.

The argument had abruptly resurfaced.

Bea was dismayed to see the information she'd wretchedly failed to get across earlier now hit her father like the end of a flicked sheet.

'It sounds very much as if your daughter's taken your advice about giving up the job, Kit.' Jenny broke the tense silence between father and daughter.

Kit thumped a colander on the table, sending up spray.

'Why did you allow me to think you were staying, Bea?' he demanded.

'I only decided to go yesterday!'

Kit fell into a seat beside Jenny.

'Can I get this straight?' he asked, one hand to his forehead. 'You've actually given in your notice at the Beachstop?'

'Yes.' Bea stuck her hands into the pockets of her jeans.

As ever, the more heated their discussion, the less information they exchanged.

Bea wished her dad didn't look so pained. Suddenly, she longed to hug him, but she didn't want to push between him and Jenny.

'So what are your future plans?' Kit asked heavily. He got restlessly to his feet.

'I'm going to college in London, Dad,' Bea said. 'To learn how to run this sort of business properly. Like you and Mum wanted.'

'You won't change your mind again?' Kit demanded. 'About college, I mean?'

'I didn't agree with Daveth at first, but we talked and . . . well, he had some good ideas, and I made up my own mind after a lot of thought.'

'Thank goodness you listened to someone, even if it wasn't me,' Kit said, his voice still choked.

Jenny joined them and linked her arms with both.

'Jenny and I talk sometimes, too,' Bea continued, biting her lip. 'She says there are things everyone who's old enough must make up their own mind about. Everyone helped . . . you, Mum, Daveth, Jenny . . . but this time I did just that — I made up my own mind.'

Jenny's gaze moved from one to the

...ther while Bea's father stared at a point on the kitchen floor.

'I think Bea's done really well coming to her own decision, Kit,' Jenny said gently.

Kit looked up, his eyes dark.

'Oh, Dad!' Bea said, moving to hug them both. She buried her face against her dad's warm shoulder. She felt him kiss the top of her head, and smelled the fresh cucumber on his hands.

'I love you so much — you know that! But in case you hadn't noticed, I'm all grown up these days!'

Farewell

The farewell evening at the Chough began far from smoothly. Garron, who'd been about his own affairs outside all afternoon, had insisted on fixing the Chough sign in place to stop it swinging in the wind.

'It's dangerous, Jenny! Near rusted away in parts. And with people coming and the wind getting up . . . '

Gary and Garron between them had clipped the poor old bird's wings. It looked a bit forlorn afterwards.

There were so many preparations to make.

An hour later, a troop of people entered the Chough carrying drums, guitars, a flute, a keyboard, stands, boxes, two fiddles and a concertina. Jenny stopped cleaning the counter long enough to read *Cady's Cousins* on the side of one case, but the name

…dn't register with her. The Cousins grinned happily at her as if they all knew her. It was most confusing.

'Come on through!' Garron called to them from the terrace. When Jenny turned, cloth still in hand, he winked broadly.

'What have you been up to, Dad?' she demanded, as the players filed past. She suddenly recognised one of her son's old friends and smiled at him.

'Nothing!' her father replied, waving an airy hand. 'Gary and me . . . thought we'd like a bit o' music, see? We reckoned it'd suit the new Chough handsome. Didn't want to bother you with the details, Jenny, as you've been that busy packing and such!'

Jenny wanted to ask more, but her father had hurried away.

Mystery

'Kerensa?' Jenny caught her daughter-in-law's arm in passing. 'Did you know about this?'

'Sort of . . . ' Kerensa admitted. 'I do love to hear Gary sing!'

Jenny nodded, a lump arriving unbidden in her throat. She loved to listen to her son, too, and soon he would be leaving. She scrubbed harder at a stubborn mark on the counter.

'All the lads together to say goodbye — just for us!' Kerensa rejoiced. 'Isn't that great? And maybe they'll be here more often now, who knows?'

'Still looking forward to moving?' Jenny asked.

'To our new place? Oh, yes!' Kerensa replied, her face alight.

'Not that I don't like the Chough!' the young woman added quickly. 'We shall be something smaller at the new place, it's true, Jenny . . . but . . . '

'It'll be your own,' Jenny said, smiling. 'I understand.'

Kerensa gave Jenny a sudden hug.

'Ben will cause us hullaballoos if we don't visit!'

Jenny looked into Kerensa's round, blue eyes, and hugged her back.

'Settle yourselves first,' she said comfortably. 'But come to see us when you can! I'm going to miss you all so much.'

'Have you been outside yet, Mum?' Gary asked on his way through the kitchen. 'Granfer's put lanterns and decorations everywhere!'

Jenny rolled her eyes in mock exasperation, and arranged the last of Lily Pinch's fairings on a large plate. The enthusiasm of her son and her father was definitely catching.

'I'll see them soon!' She held out two plates. 'Gary, take these to a table, will you?'

'I'll go upstairs to check on the baby now, Jenny,' Kerensa said.

'I think we're as ready as we'll ever be down here!'

Kind of Blue

Drying her hands on a kitchen towel, Jenny had one last mission before she changed for the evening. She slipped outside and gazed up. Her painted crow, the Chough's long-standing sign and famous Cornish emblem, with his sharp eye, ruffled black feathers and his even-more-faded red leg, was still, held by Garron's makeshift binding. Jenny had the oddest idea in her head that he was waiting for something.

'Is it any wonder you look as if you're trying hard to make the best of it,' she murmured gently. 'But there are real, live choughs come back to Cornwall now, my handsome! So we mustn't ever give up, must we?'

She badly wanted any restoration to preserve her feathered friend's present dignity, and that meant asking an expert. Eventually, Jenny stood back and rolled down the sleeves of her overall. She'd come to a decision at last. She would ask Kit for help.

With a sigh of relief, she hurried back inside.

Jenny had bought a pretty blouse for the evening. It was hanging outside her bedroom wardrobe to keep it pristine. Blue suited her, Kit had once said, and, of course, since then she'd found it her favourite colour. As she lifted the blouse on to her bed, a thread from one sleeve caught against her silver bracelet. She tugged at it lightly. To her dismay, the clasp gave way and broke. If only she'd been more careful!

But what once might have felt like a disaster was now only a regret. The bracelet was Dan's treasured gift, but tonight . . . tonight of all nights, she wouldn't be able wear it. Perhaps, with Kit arriving soon, that was as it should be.

Carefully, Jenny unhooked the last of the thread. Then she slipped the bracelet into a small cloth bag and placed it carefully in her dressing-table drawer.

Loving memories of Dan would dwell unchanged in her heart always. But her life was taking a new direction now, and there was no changing that, either. The blue blouse felt soft as she buttoned it, and fitted perfectly.

Absent Friends

Jenny stood at the foot of the stairs, listening to Gary and his friends launch into 'Going Up Camborne Hill'. Kit still hadn't arrived.

'Jenny . . . hi!' It was Paul, with Sally beside him. 'Two of my favourite people!' he said, sweeping both women into the old, unembarrassed bear-hug.

'Watch out . . . Jenny's all dressed up!' Sally giggled.

'Is Kit here?' Paul asked, smiling.

'He promised he'd come,' Jenny said.

'Bea's not here yet, either,' Sally said, looking round.

At that moment, there was an excited scream from Ben.

'Bee-triss!'

Jenny's grandson skidded across the hallway on his knees. Laughing, Bea picked him up.

'Is Kit . . . ?' Jenny tried to ask,

looking past Bea to the door.

But Daveth was already beckoning. Bea had moved off with Ben still in her arms, leaving Jenny's question unheard.

Jenny found seats for Paul's parents, Morwenna and Bob, and brought them sandwiches. She helped Lily hand plates of food around. She managed to pour coffee for herself, and took time out to hear Gary sing two sea-shanties. She even joined with everyone else in two rousing choruses of 'Trelawney', exchanging smiles with Sally when Paul sang, as ever, in the Key of Biddick.

But later, when the music softened, and the songs carried words to wish Gary and his family well for their future, she turned away. Not because she didn't want to send her son off in a good heart, but because suddenly, painfully, she longed for Kit's presence.

The music quickened again, and Bea whirled past.

'He said he'd be here as soon as he could!' she managed breathlessly in answer to Jenny's question as she spun past.

Jenny leaned against her new door-frame, between the old Chough and the new terrace, glad everyone was enjoying themselves, but wretchedly unwilling to telephone Trenfos.

She watched Kerensa slip down the stairs and hug Gary as they met. Her daughter-in-law turned in Jenny's direction and smiled, resting her head on her two folded hands to indicate the baby was sleeping well, despite the party. Looking out across the terrace, Jenny smiled to see her father. It looked as if he was enjoying his dance with Lily out there.

Escape

Among the buzz of noise and chatter, Jenny felt rather than heard a movement behind her. Another step, and Kit came into view.

'I'm so sorry I'm late.'

'Is anything wrong?' Jenny asked, searching his face.

She disentangled herself from one of Garron's extravagant decorations and slipped her arm through his.

'Not exactly . . . ' Kit muttered. 'I asked Bea to let you know I'd be coming . . . ' he added defensively.

Jenny bit her lip.

'I'm not getting at you,' she said. 'It's been everything at once, hasn't it? First, we were so worried about Ben. Then I was involved with getting the family to pack for the move . . . and then I got all worried about advising Bea. Especially in case you thought I'd been interfering!'

'It didn't make for a good atmosphere that time you came to Trenfos . . . not for serious talking, anyway,' Kit said.

'And this evening?' Jenny asked.

Kit pushed a hand through his hair and sighed.

'This evening, Melissa rang. She was worried about everything. Where Bea would live now she's decided she wants to find somewhere for herself in London, how she would manage, what did I think of this qualification she was aiming for . . . Mel gets so upset by changes of plan, even though Bea has decided to carry on her studies as we both wanted.'

He glanced at Jenny unhappily.

'I didn't mean you to come second to Melissa, tonight of all nights. Are you upset?'

'I'm just glad you're here,' Jenny said, leaning her head on his shoulder. 'It's important you should talk to Bea's mother. I know you'd support me if Gary ever needed my help.'

The music and singing rose again.

'I . . . I've been hoping all week to have time alone,' Kit said, moving closer so Jenny could hear him.

'Let's escape somewhere quieter,' she suggested, taking his hand.

★ ★ ★

They wove their way through the crowd and, in the deepening dusk, reached the far corner of the terrace where there were more shadows than lanterns. The air rose coolly from the grass below.

Cady's Cousins announced a short break for refreshments, promising to return for a finale. In the lull, the sound of Penarren's stream chuckled just above the more distant whisper of the sea.

'There's something missing out here,' Kit said suddenly.

'It's our awful squeak,' Jenny said. 'The sign's giving up the ghost, so Dad silenced it.'

'That's too bad.' Kit's gaze became

very focused. 'What have you decided about the Chough?' he asked.

'I need it properly repaired as befits our dear old bird,' Jenny said. 'You said I could ask you . . . ?'

'Correction. I *wanted* you to ask me. Long ago!' Kit's voice held a smile.

'Thank you.' Jenny kissed his cheek. 'I'm glad that's settled!

'Have you seen your daughter enjoying herself?' she went on. 'This evening will be her farewell to Penarren, as well as Gary's.'

'Bea recovers from our arguments more quickly than I do!' Kit said ruefully.

'I was sorry I didn't manage to warn you that she'd spoken to me first. I ought to have done.'

'What I'm battling with now is the dreaded realisation that my only daughter doesn't need me any longer . . . '

Jenny folded her hands with Kit's as they gazed into the dusk.

'She might not need you in the old way, my dear. Just as Gary hasn't needed me for a long while! But families always need each other occasionally.'

'Will we ever stop worrying about our children?' Kit asked.

'Perhaps we should worry about each other instead.' Jenny stirred some fine gravel against the wall with an increasingly restless foot. 'I don't think it would be selfish to put into words what we want for the future.'

Kit held Jenny and smiled into her eyes. She gazed steadily back.

'Isn't it time we did, my love?' she asked softly.

'It is,' he murmured. 'Look, now . . . '

Joy Be With You All

He turned her gently into the circle of his arms, so she rested against him and could follow his gaze. At the head of the valley a few trees crouched as if a strong wind always blew. Above the leaning branches rose a fat, copper-coloured moon. It seemed to bounce once on the edge of the earth, then fall upwards into the purple sky. The grasses rustled, then stilled.

'I want us to have time for each other always and every day,' Kit murmured. 'Jenny, my sweetheart, will you marry me?'

'Yes . . . ' she whispered, moon-gazing one heartbeat longer.

From indoors, and the rooms full of voices and the warmth of friends, Garron Trelawney's voice called out for 'A toast to the *Etta*, my 'andsomes, and the dear old Chough!'

Jenny twisted in Kit's light embrace and drew his face to hers.

'Of course I'll marry you, Kit Venning.'

He returned her loving smile, and his arms locked her close.

Their children had bid already for their futures. With this warm kiss, Jenny and Kit at last made their own claim on hope, and love.

After a while, the music began again, steadied, and gained a lilt. The band sang the 'Farewell Shanty'. There was a ripple of applause, then Gary's clear tenor began the song 'Goodnight, And Joy Be With You All'.

We do hope that you have enjoyed reading this large print book.

Did you know that all of our titles are available for purchase?

We publish a wide range of high quality large print books including:
Romances, Mysteries, Classics
General Fiction
Non Fiction and Westerns

Special interest titles available in large print are:
The Little Oxford Dictionary
Music Book, Song Book
Hymn Book, Service Book

Also available from us courtesy of Oxford University Press:
Young Readers' Dictionary
(large print edition)
Young Readers' Thesaurus
(large print edition)

For further information or a free brochure, please contact us at:
Ulverscroft Large Print Books Ltd.,
The Green, Bradgate Road, Anstey,
Leicester, LE7 7FU, England.
Tel: (00 44) **0116 236 4325**
Fax: (00 44) **0116 234 0205**

NO MISTAKING LOVE

Moyra Tarling

Working at Moonbeam Lake, it wasn't easy for single mother Laura Matthews. She wanted her twins to enjoy summer in the place she'd once loved — despite its painful memories. But she hadn't counted on Tanner Mcleod's reappearance. Six years ago, she'd comforted him when his brother died, and it had led to passion. But Tanner had left before she'd discovered the consequences of their love. How could she confess that *he* was the father the twins had never met?

KNAVE OF DIAMONDS

Wendy Kremer

Sharon is employed by a retailer to write some PR text about Patrick, a famous jewellery designer, who's creating an exclusive collection for the everyday woman. Patrick's initial resentment of Sharon changes when he gets to know her, whilst she admits that he's a fascinating man. If only other women didn't think so too! Then as Sharon and Patrick visit Hong Kong for a photo session things begin to buzz — only to fall apart. What has fate designed for them?